E1.50

FAREN MILLER

WARNER BOOKS

A Time Warner Company

WARNER BOOKS EDITION

Copyright © 1991 by Faren Miller
All rights reserved.

Questar® is a registered trademark of Warner Books, Inc.

Cover illustration by Gary Ruddell
Cover design by Don Puckey

Warner Books, Inc.
666 Fifth Avenue
New York, NY 10103

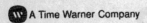 A Time Warner Company

Printed in the United States of America

First Printing: March, 1991

10 9 8 7 6 5 4 3 2 1

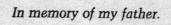

In memory of my father.

Prologue: The Artifact

The winter rain came down strongly, soaking darkness into the stones, cascading from rooftops to the streets where puddles joined and became rivulets in the High City, muddy torrents below, as they swept up debris from the alleys around the great markets and spun it farther down the spiraling maze of roads, lanes, and stairways covering the slopes of Xalycis Rock. In the warrens of Tumbleside, beggars jostled for shelter, but some would die of exposure before morning, as surely as winter winds brought rain, summer winds sand.

It was the rats and a bad dream that drove Ragman over the wall of rubble and into the Tumbles themselves. The squeak and scurry roused him. Water foamed around the steps beneath the doorway where he had fallen asleep. In the dream, a mob had pursued him, clamoring for his blood, through the familiar turnings of Low City and Tumbleside, and he could find no hiding place. As he woke now to the rush of rain, a thought came to Ragman: No one would follow him into the ruins. There was plenty of high ground there, roofs piled on roofs since the day it all came down, centuries past. Before the downpour could wash the last fragments of his dream away, he was sliding down the far side of the barrier where Tumbles and Tumbleside met, heading for the hulk of the vast, slumped structure that dominated the no-man's-land.

By some miracle, he reached his goal without falling head-long into one of the crevices that seamed the debris. Numb and exhausted, he crawled into a man-sized opening between two broken pillars projecting from the great mound. Then he dozed for a time. There were no rats here and no dreams—unless he dreamed the light before he opened his eyes and saw it, a faint glow from behind him, like a candle burning low in a room where the air was calm and steady. Oblivious to the crowding stones and, as he wriggled deeper in, dust from the last shifting of the rubble, Ragman made his way to the place where thick walls had collapsed inward to leave an open space beneath.

The shining came from a rounded thing protruding from a mound of debris and drift-sand. He crawled toward it staring, paying no mind to the sharp stones that grated against his knees and hands. The light sang in his head. Treasure. As he began to dig, sand poured and glittered, a spill of gold, a promise. Beneath, the object was caught fast. Ragman pawed through the rubble to free it, muttering broken phrases, coughing from the lungs when the dust flew.

The debris felt strange, as though he scooped handfuls of insects. Puzzled, he stopped his frantic digging for a moment. A pebble slid down into his palm. Before he could toss it away, it *flowed*. He held a chunk of ice—a mass of wet clay—a gnarled burl of old wood. Ragman whimpered and dropped it, prepared to flee. But the light pulsed from the buried globe, distracting him. Nearly there. *Treasure*.

It held all his attention now. Shape-shifting stones meant

nothing. Maybe he had once seen one in a market stall, going through its paces while a crone whined "Relicts, relicts, sers, five orrins for a marvel from the past!" But Ragman's memories had melted in the rain.

There, he had it. Though it glowed so bright he had to squint, the globe felt cool as a wine jar. If he could have found an opening, he would have raised it to his lips. How would it feel to drink down heaven? The light dimmed a little, and his wild elation began to recede. They'd envy him. They'd *want* it, all of them. Oh, but he'd sell it dear. Give me all the orrins in the world and maybe, maybe, I'll let you touch it.

Deep in his layers of filthy, raveling tunics and leggings and scraps, Ragman had a secret pouch, empty now except for stale crumbs and a forgotten copper. Trembling, he wrapped the globe in one of his bits of cloth and thrust it in, tight against his belly. The light died as if he'd gone blind, but the promise surged in his blood. *Treasure . . . magic!*

Two days later, Ragman would lie dead in a waste pit, throat slashed and an orrin still clutched in his hand. More orrins, more blood, would mark the globe's passage between owners, on its way from Tumbleside to High Xalycis—a place much changed since men first made and used the Artifact. For the mages of Xalycis were long gone.

I

The Percept's Flaw

Stilpin of Xalycis, to Caravan Master Robellac—

Esteemed master: May you be in your usual good health when this reaches you. First, assurances—all is well. The dyers have made fine work of the Arahan silk, and it goes to the weavers in three days. When you return next spring, you will have hangings fit for the gods.

A remarkable thing has happened. Some Tumbleside villain came up to the Market with a wild tale of finding a bit of mage-work that isn't a mere relict but an Artifact entire. (I suspect he had "found" it at knife point.) You may say it takes a brave fool to speak of mages when we've been trying to forget them for two hundred years. The place for a relict is a cult-den or the back room of an oddshop, not the auction floor. As for this so-called Artifact . . . well, I am getting ahead of myself. To resume: The villain sidled in, looking for an agent to sell his trove. Hadthar was willing to give it a try (anything for an orrin or a laugh), but Ser Tumbleside spooked at the last minute. Next thing we know, the mage-work turns up in Council Hall, no less. It's a Civic Treasure; the mages were "misunderstood."

Typical Council nonsense. Their notion of history is last year's name-day banquet or last season's mistress. And what did they do with their new Civic Treasure? Put it up on a pillar for the world to gawp at, or sling it into the cellars with the old shields and war banners? No, our estimable leaders turned around and sold the damned thing to Aubric i-Arnix, for a rumored twenty thousand!

Much wailing and gnashing of teeth around the Market, when we heard the news. From suspect sorcerous rubbish to Arnix treasure within two weeks, and none of us made a bent copper on the deal! Only the meddling of demons could produce such a set-down for the trade. "But, Stilpin," you will protest, "commerce is the gods' great invention." No one can doubt that, in this City of a Thousand Temples, especially with the fabulous example of Robellac's Luck to remind us. So, then. Perhaps some of that Luck has rubbed off—or the Lady of the Rock whispered in my ear. While the Market still sat under its cloud of gloom, I went out to the back streets and bought a half-dozen relicts. The usual sort of stuff—a roof tile that drips blood, a tangle of wire and string that shrieks like a girl if you pick it up. Broken magic, old horrors.

Who would want such trash? *Arnix will*, when he needs another Artifact and there's none to be had. Remember when you got him to buying snowlands amber? He must still have a hundredweight somewhere in his vaults. With your leave, I'll buy more relicts and put together a nice little collection for the Grand Collector. Maybe it will spark a Wallwalk fad.

Your servant,
Stilpin

Caravan Master Robellac, to his agent Stilpin of Xalycis:

It's fitting that you wrote of Robellac's Luck in that extraordinary letter. But you must be patient, my boy, for I have news of my own to tell before I give you your answer.

Here in Prak Eda, a miserable village of extortionate sheepherders clustered round a well, I have struck treasure as rich as your Artifact. Nay, richer, for this is no mere bauble for the Arnix Vaults. Can you guess what I have found? No, impossible!

Having formed the idea of obtaining a supply of the local carpets (magnificent as the people are crude), I visited Prak Eda's sole merchant bank in quest of a scribe to witness a written contract—an object these mostly unlettered folk regard with both suspicion and some awe. The staff at this establishment consisted of one palsied ancient, a jug-eared boy, and a female who (gods be thanked) appeared to have her wits about her. I was on the point of hiring her when the old man tugged at my sleeve, mumbling something I couldn't make out. We went a little apart, and he proceeded to tell me that the girl was bewitched. Good at languages, aye, she had a dozen at her command, and wrote a neat enough hand, but I must beware for she was apt to "go strange." As I was preparing to demand what he meant, the girl came up to us and said, "If you must hear ill of me, let me tell it myself. I'm a failed percept."

Well, that took me aback! Everyone's heard tales of the northern kings with their percept-counselors and percept-bards. When these "fail," they're said to be creatures of unluck, silent when called upon most urgently, or prone to fits of madness. Yet the powers of a percept to engage and assimilate the most complex situation, to see clear where others are all astray—that is a wondrous thing. I asked this self-proclaimed failure if she had been a bard. No: she was of the other sort.

It came to me that this honesty was her odd manner of wooing me, for life in Prak Eda cannot be pleasant for one used to better. She would leap at the chance of joining my company, take her where it might. My instinct was all atwitch and it was as much as I could do to keep from dashing off to consult the beads then and there. At this very moment, your courier found me! The gods could give no clearer message.

So it is that I send to you not only a bank draft for five thousand Xalycan orrins, but the percept herself. (You see how the gods have watched over your enterprises this time!) She tells me her name is Moabet Shar. I leave her in your care, knowing your happy talent for dealing with womankind. She will report upon the situation in Xalycis and, I dare to hope, *predict its future turnings*.

Be kind to the girl. She is far from home.

Yours in hope,
Robellac

"She's *here*?" Stilpin groped for his boots and tried, one-handed, to do up his tunic.

"Just outside, sir. A bit tired, with the traveling and all."

"Great bloody hells, that's all I need! Some creature out of a fairy tale, and damaged goods at that—"

"Quiet little thing," the courier put in. "Not like my daughters, gabbling all the day till a man can't think straight."

Stilpin had pulled on his boots, run a hand through his dark, unruly hair, and given up on the obstinate tunic laces. After a bad meal, worse wine, and unspeakable boredom in the company of an oddshop dealer, his head ached, and the triumph of buying an extravagant "cloud-feather" relict had palled. "I don't suppose she's pretty, this percept."

The man shrugged. "Looks a bit like my youngest, she does. But quieter."

With a sigh, Stilpin drew himself up. "You'd better bring her in."

The courier returned accompanied by a small figure in plain traveling clothes. A scarf hid the hair. Pointed nose, peeling with sunburn. Narrow chin, arched brows—a fox face, unsmiling.

"Sera—Shar, is it? Welcome to Xalycis," Stilpin declared with what warmth he could muster.

She turned and looked straight at him then, with a vast, brown-amber stare that made him instantly conscious of his stubbled jaw, his wrinkled clothes, his youth. Where had he faced such a gaze before? Bas-Imret, of course, carved from granite in the Temple of Birds, human limbs and the head of a falcon, set with topaz eyes. By torchlight, they would seem to follow you . . . .

She broke into his reverie. "And you are Stilpin, Master Robellac's man." Moabet Shar sank into a cushioned chair as though she wished never to move again. Scuffed boots showed under her long coat.

"I'll be on my way," the courier said. Thus prompted, Stilpin sent the man off, with a ten-orrin tip that brought a grin to the weathered face.

Then there was nothing for it. Stilpin must make conversation with Robellac's falcon-girl, or die in the attempt. He stumbled through a few trivial exchanges (Had she eaten? Yes, at the inn down the street), winced at the thought of trying his charm on her, and was on the point of giving up in despair when she asked him about his strategy in the relict hunt.

"Have the dealers caught on to what you're doing yet?"

From the moment he began to answer to the point where his voice grew raw with talking, Stilpin forgot about resentment, weariness, or mistrust—scarcely knew she was there, for she did not coax or interrogate but simply listened. Like drylands soaking up the rain, that silence, missing nothing.

He stopped at last, astonished. "How did you do that?"

Of course she understood, but Moabet was tired enough to yield to impulse and teased him with a solemn face: "A binding spell. One of the first things they teach us is the Compelling Art."

Wonderful, the stark horror on his face.

She relented. "Actually, it wasn't. I was interested and didn't interrupt—that's all it takes."

Stilpin peered at her narrowly. "No spells?"

"I swear it."

Disarmed, he failed to question her about that mysterious "flaw" she had confessed in Prak Eda.

Stilpin had found her a sleeping mat and blankets, provided her with candles, pen, and paper as well, and gone to his own rooms near Robellac's warehouse-offices, before he remembered what he had meant to ask. *Damnation.* That had been his best chance to play the blunt employer and say straight out, "What's wrong with you?" He rubbed his rasping chin, then swore aloud, with greater feeling. Somehow he knew: Robellac had not asked her either.

Wind whipped the percept's gown about her ankles. She gave the dull blue wool an impatient tug and crossed the platform to join Stilpin. They stood at the top of an old watchtower on a spur of Xalycis Rock overlooking rooftops, gardens, temple spires, and the huddled buildings of Low City; beyond, the flat, hazed expanse of plains paled into desert at the horizon.

"Perfect lair for a robber king, back in the Warring Times." Stilpin gestured toward the plains, where the caravan road made a white arc between greening fields. "Swoop down, commit a little mayhem, and back you go to the Rock where no sane army would follow. Fortress Xalycis. Later the merchants soft-talked their way in and it all opened up. Abassi, Rhos, Shandar, Thrani, there's whole towns and tribes within the city, and they brought all their gods with them."

"And those gods are still here, while the mages—vanished." She made a fluttering gesture with one hand, as though the sorcerers of Xalycis might have flown away into that sky where now a lone hawk circled, black against brightness.

Stilpin thought of something he'd heard from some caravan drover. "Did they go up north to become scholars, bards . . . percepts?"

She favored him with an odd smile, more sour than sweet. "So I should rejoice in my homecoming?" The percept shook her head. "I'm a stranger in your city. If I seem to take on its ways too quickly"—again that smile—"remember: I listen."

She did more than that, as he discovered when they made their way to the bazaars of the Lesser Market. Amid the din of hammers on metal, blades thudding into butchers' blocks, peddlers calling their wares, and a tumult of voices in different tongues, Stilpin nearly forgot that she walked beside him. He was teasing a buxom amulet seller, his fingers at the loose collar of her robe, when she looked over his shoulder and said, "That new clerk of yours talks hand-cant faster than you, love."

He swung around. Moabet was engaged in lively, almost silent conversation with a grinning bondsman, fingers flashing in the mute speech servants used for their private gossip. He caught the signs for "money" and "women" before the bondsman shoved hands in pockets and ducked back into the crowd.

Stilpin had the uncomfortable feeling they'd been discussing him. Biting back a sarcastic remark, he began to watch the percept's every move. There was the listening of course, to conversations in a dozen tongues. More striking, though, was the way her glance would sweep the scenes around her, lighting on details. What had caught her attention? A booth of intricately braided ropes, a family of beggars, a quarrel among porters, a rich man's palanquin . . . he could not follow it all.

When friends noticed him in the crowd, they wondered at his preoccupied expression. Robellac must be pushing his agent too hard, they thought. Look how he walked right by the jeweler's girl (prettiest piece in Xalycis, clad in nothing but bangles under her cloak), and neglected to rub the Hearth God's belly for luck when he passed the statue on his way to the Eastern Gate. Off to deal with the Thrani no doubt, poor devil.

Stilpin had bought two of the meat pies known as "turtles" and a bag of oranges. They ate as they walked, leaving the market squares just after the midday bell boomed its single note.

The Thrani Quarter was a tangled maze of alleys running between high stone walls. A few doorways lurked in dark recesses like eyes in deep sockets. From the upper stories, screened windows thrust outward, echoing the forms of dovecotes resting on each flat roof. The unseen birds' cooing and fluttering sounded unnaturally loud, for the Thrani were silent folk. Veiled women glided past, anklets faintly chiming. Men gathered in brooding groups, puffing long clay pipes painted yellow or scarlet. Even the children played their games in flurries of hand-cant, with the rare, fluting cry of victory.

Stilpin halted before a doorway with an iron grill and a dangling bell-rope.

"Now, for the misdirection," he murmured. "This is a spice merchant's shop. The customer is expected to haggle and drink thimbles of tea for half the afternoon." He tugged on the rope and waited.

At last the grill creaked open and a robed figure beckoned them in, to shadows heavy with the odors of cinnamon, saffron, and dust. Coins changed hands; moments later, Stilpin and Moabet were blinking in daylight again, behind the shop.

He led the way across a cracked stone courtyard flourishing with weeds, to an equally neglected garden, and on to a final door so low he had to bow his head to enter.

A solemn child ushered them into a surprisingly opulent room, its every surface carved, painted, or padded with soft velvet.

"Who is the woman?" The young man reclining on a couch was dressed as richly as his surroundings. It seemed as though some piece of the furnishings had spoken.

"My clerk. You know the power of written words to refresh the memory. We shall come to an agreement today." Stilpin sprawled in a chair and eyed the prospective relict seller. "You haven't changed your mind?"

The young man winced at such un-Thrani bluntness. He paid no further heed to the clerk perched cross-legged on an ottoman behind her master, as he sought to introduce the conversation into more acceptable channels of vague flattery and vaguer hints of future mutual profit.

Servants brought tea and cloying sweets, attending the men

and ignoring the female clerk. She listened, hands neatly in her lap. Stilpin felt her gaze at the back like the pressure of cool fingers. It made him clumsy; he gave up more than he had planned to pay for the Thrani's relict, a broken statue's hand, marble flickering with ghost-lights. Was the thing any more than rubble fit for the midden?

"It's wondrous," she said softly as they made their way back to Robellac's warehouse.

"Too damned expensive," he muttered. "I rushed it."

"You'll attract more sellers if they think they can outsmart you. They're fools, though, to sell at all."

Stilpin stopped and turned to look at her. They were on a stair cut into the Rock, linking two streets, no one in earshot. "Why? Do you know of a use for the things? They're like spearheads from an old battle—people collect those too. But we started this war and lost it, right here in Xalycis."

"True magic. Even the scattered bits the mages left behind are beautiful."

Her words made him squirm as though she stood there in her prim blue gown and mouthed obscenities. His own growing fascination with the relicts disturbed him. If Aubric i-Arnix wanted to dabble in mage-work, that was nothing to Stilpin. Trade is trade. But "true magic" . . . and a percept here at his side. Was some sorcerer's ghost watching him now, laughing?

Over the next days, Stilpin grew used to her and managed to dismiss his qualms. Caught up in the grand game of opening negotiations with Arnix (his private image was of a lion hunt, Arnix the golden quarry), he passed the percept some of his ordinary workload, gave her a place among his clerks, and read her reports with an absentminded pleasure in their competence. When the lion was trapped, the deal all but concluded, he did not give a second thought to bringing her with him to Arnix House.

Clad soberly but well, they came to High Xalycis in a hired palanquin, the choicest of the relicts resting beside them in a specially made box—impervious, Stilpin hoped, to seeping magical effusions.

Late-afternoon sunlight gilded the majestic facades of the Wallwalk mansions and gleamed on the strings of ancestral banner-balls hanging from their high roof peaks. A light wind roused faint harmonies, a solemn jangling.

Servants showed them in, more servants smoothly took charge of the precious box, and a further retinue brought them to the surprisingly austere room where Aubric i-Arnix conducted business.

From Arnix's arrival to the final flourish of Moabet's pen, Stilpin was in a state of controlled tension, like an acrobat poised on a tightrope, juggling torches. He could have wept with relief when it was done.

Arnix was pleased. Beneath the bristling gray brows, his eyes gleamed. Massive as he was, he stepped lightly, chatting of one thing and another, always returning to gaze at the relicts again.

"You must stay to dinner," he said. "You and—" he gestured toward Moabet without looking at her. "We dine early, in the old manner."

"We would be honored," Stilpin replied.

But Arnix had already made a sign of dismissal, and the parade of servants began once more, ushering merchant and clerk through the bewildering expanse of the great house.

There were seven at table that evening. A young Council member and his wife, new to Arnix House and innocently unaware of their role as "easy meat" in the coming conversation; an Arnix niece, deputizing for her uncle's perpetually ailing wife; Stilpin and his clerk, unknown factors who might provide fresh amusement if the Councilman palled; and Hendor Ebrin, the Vinculine, governor of Low Xalycis and honored adversary—present where his lady was barred, for Aubric held decided views on that ancient scandal, forgiving the seducer but not the disgraced wife.

The Councilman lasted through the first three courses, prattling blithely in the beginning, oblivious to his host's sarcastic encouragements, until the Vinculine plied his wit and left the victim hamstrung, gazing about him blankly as his wife clutched his hand. Talk ceased for the roast goose, superb in a sauce of fiery spices that brought some color back to the Councilman's cheeks. Arnix, scarlet and sweating, looked up from his plate only when the last bones were stripped.

''Your other guests are new to me.'' The Vinculine indicated Stilpin and Moabet.

Stilpin straightened in his chair, ready to face the first assault with an air of courage.

But Arnix's mood had changed. ''Robellac's young man. Stands to make a whacking profit from me,'' he said genially. Then allowed a tantalizing silence to lengthen.

The Vinculine's prominent eyes hooded. His mouth, grotesquely wide in a face too small for its heavy features, curved into a smile of purest charm. ''It *has* been a good year for the trade. Prosperous times for all Xalycis.''

Not quite true that last, and maddeningly provocative to a man who now owned the Artifact and a select group of relicts. Aubric i-Arnix did not want to talk about the fortunes of the trade, when his own was so much more splendid.

''Such platitudes, Hendor,'' he drawled. ''Are you angling for a high priesthood?''

The great men grinned at each other like beasts baring

fangs. The Arnix niece looked nervous, though she had witnessed such displays since earliest childhood.

The Vinculine made ironic concession to his host. "Tell us, then, Aubric, what has the young man sold you?"

"Would you like to see?" Arnix beckoned to the Vinculine, pointedly excluding his other guests. "We'll be a few moments."

Stilpin relaxed fractionally when they had left the room, though he would have liked a glimpse of the Artifact. He wondered if even the Vinculine was permitted into its presence.

Haltingly, the remaining guests revived the conversation. Stilpin and Moabet took little part—they were, after all, scarcely better than the servants who moved around the table like shadows or soft winds, bearing wine, fresh napkins, orange-water in silver bowls.

At last Arnix returned, a silent Vinculine coming after. The host's high spirits seemed to eclipse Hendor Ebrin now. Arnix roared for more wine (the serving man at his elbow, decanter poised, did not turn a hair), then crowed with delight as the final course appeared, a spectacular dish that he dearly loved, "Burning Ramparts": a concoction of cakes, glazes, and decorative ranks of candied fruits, soaked in liquor and set ablaze. The flames rose blue, almost transparent, quivering with every shifting current of air. In the darkened room, they had a mesmerizing glamor.

As Arnix paused, smiling with the serving knife in his hand before the ritual of making the first cut, an unfamiliar voice broke in.

"The instrument of murder is at hand." (Startled, Arnix dropped the blunt knife.) "The Lion dies, seek treasure from his tomb, a golden vengeance—"

Before Moabet could say more in that strange tranced voice that Stilpin had never heard before, Aubric's niece grasped her roughly by the arm, screaming, "Stop it! What do you mean? He won't die!" The Arnix girl broke into hysterical sobbing, fingers still gripping Moabet's brocaded sleeve until Stilpin pried them loose. He was shaking so badly he could only watch as the percept slipped sideways and fell to the floor unconscious.

II

Ladder Valley

"Hey, Dalu. Her fingers twitched! Do you think her color's better?" A familiar voice, made ragged by strain. Stilpin's breath ruffled her hair as he leaned over her.

"Looks like a live young woman, asleep."

"You said that two hours ago."

"More like three. True then, true now." Dalu—a Shandar by the name and accent—rumbling laconic responses. With her eyes still shut, she knew his expression would be deadpan, teasing.

The room reeked of chemicry. Not sick room smells or healer's herbs. Chemic. Ah, Moabet, you slowpate! Stilpin's first master, the grandee perfumer, had a chemic. Sidestep Robellac, go to ground with an old friend instead. . . . That was enough to tell her how bad things were this time. Despairing, she groaned.

"Percept?"

Her vision swam into focus. Stilpin took her hand, dropped it, scowled. He was still in his banquet finery, the worse for long wearing. Jaw stubbled, face gaunt with fatigue, fuel for anger—"Why the hell did you let me take you to that fucking dinner?"

"Easy, lad." Dalu Chemic approached with a heavy tread. A squat pure-blood Shandar: shaved skull, eyes extravagantly slanted, earlobes dangling with the weight of onyx plugs. "How's the head?"

"All right." Just throbbing with each pulsebeat.

"Can you sit?" Gently, Dalu took her by the shoulders. His hands, scarred and stained from his trade, smelled of soap, with an undertone of acrid essences.

She sat and looked around her. A small room, lamplit, whitewashed, crammed with jars, boxes, bottles, retorts, mortars, cabinets, basins, leaving barely enough room for a wooden stool and the narrow cot she now occupied. Dalu stood behind her, while Stilpin sat at the foot of the cot.

"They must fear you, Dalu Chemic. Your neighbors haven't looted this place."

Moabet was talking at random to put off the moment she dreaded, the thing she must learn, but Stilpin stiffened. "How did you know where we are?"

"Street noises," she said. Heard through the thin walls and judged unconsciously, as her mind so often worked. (Oh gods, what had she done this time?) "Too loud and disorderly for Wallwalk. A mix of accents, so it can't be the Shandar settlement. Anyway"—a glance back at Dalu—"you wouldn't mix ordinary chemicry with your priestly duties."

He drew in a hissing breath and came around to squat on his heels beside the cot, eyes narrowed to thin creases in the flesh. Then, strangely, Dalu smiled. "Wise little witch. Have you met a drum-priest of the Roan Horse Mystery before?" He raised his arms so the sleeves fell back from the intricate tattoos that extended nearly to his shoulders.

"Blessed be the Mare," she replied in his own language.

"Are you through showing off?" Stilpin cut in. "I can see how you dazzled Master Robellac, but he missed the big event at Arnix House tonight. Pity."

Moabet closed her eyes. She would not weep in the presence of strangers. Her head ached miserably now, and her hands had grown cold. "You'll have to tell me. When the fit comes, I never remember it afterward. What did I say?"

With clerkly exactitude, Stilpin gave her back her own lost words. Cryptic, bardic, disastrous.

She muttered a very ordinary oath. Looked up, eyes burning, swung her arm—but he caught it before it could slam into the wall. "Haven't you done enough harm already?"

"What do you care what I do to myself? The contract's void, isn't it?"

"No."

Astonishment comes rarely to a percept, even to one with a ruinous flaw. Three times before, she had suffered the fit, faced men's fear and anger, and managed somehow to escape with her life. "What do you mean?"

He maintained his grip on her arm. "Let's say Arnix dies, as you seem to have predicted. What happens then?"

"If they catch me, I'll be burnt as a death-witch."

"Not to you, damn it. To the city."

Well, that was obvious enough. "Rumors, factions, hysteria. A move in Council to ban relicts—countered by the fascination with the old magic, what's left of it."

"And the Artifact?"

More obvious still. "Why d'you think Arnix will be killed?"

"The murderer will have it." Gazing at nothing, deep in thought, Stilpin had loosened his hold on her, but his fingers tapped a restless rhythm on her arm. He must use his mistresses like worry beads. When he spoke again, his voice seemed to come from a distance. "The gods know I'm no hero."

Dalu asked sharply, "What do you mean to do?"

"Do? Nothing much." Stilpin gave a joyless laugh. "Watch Xalycis seethe like a kicked anthill, and make Robellac his profit."

"You don't need me for that," Moabet said.

"Ah, but I might."

"So, you're the kind of man who collects string and scrapes the ink off vellum to save a few coppers." She had never spoken so rudely to an employer. Prudent, humble Moabet Shar was no use to her now, faced with this stubborn clerk. She had to get away. "Get it through your head, man, if I stay here after Arnix dies, I'm dead. Do you want to be caught in the mess that will follow?"

Stilpin was looking at the Shandar.

The chemic/priest looked back for a long moment, then nodded. "She'll be safe in Ladder Valley. City guards don't come down there. Villains keep away." He gave a wolfish grin. "We have strong gods and sharp knives."

"I'm an outsider," she protested.

"You speak like a native," Stilpin countered. "Better than I do, and they let me run loose in the Valley one summer when I was a boy."

Patterns settled into place, distracting her from her apprehensions. Stilpin the young 'prentice scribe with an aloof master. In the past days, she had caught references to Etroren i-Vuorn, the Wallwalk perfumer—a dry-fish cuckold who'd lost his wife to the Vinculine. A boy in that household would hunger for kindness, for a hero and protector. "All right," she said, before she was aware of making the decision. "I'll go." And to Dalu, "I'm in your debt."

"Stilpin will collect." A wicked side glance at the clerk.

Stilpin reddened, but had no chance to reply. The sounds outside had grown louder—rough shouts, as a fight spilled from tavern to street. A woman was screaming abuse, a crescendo of obscenities culminating with a shrieked "Mage-lover!" A cry that had not been heard in Xalycis for well over a century.

"It's beginning." Moabet surveyed the room, which seemed fragile as an eggshell, no haven now. "How long before they look for substitute mages as their scapegoats? Chemics, perfumers, scholars. Percepts. You won't be safe here, Dalu."

"Move operations to the Valley?" Stilpin asked him.

The Shandar wore a fearsome scowl. "Curse the day we left the roads. All my life I've loved Ladder Valley, but you know what it is, boy? Stone wagons and painted horses. What kind of priesthood abandons its herds?"

"What kind of citizen writes off his city at the first sign of danger?"

The two men glared at each other.

Moabet let the silence lengthen, until they became aware of her again. Both had the grace to look embarrassed.

"The brawl *outside* has moved off," she said. "You're sure you weren't followed when you brought me here?"

Stilpin nodded. "Arnix was too busy blustering to fear you yet. That kind thinks he's immortal. We came here in a hire-palanquin, with none the wiser." He became brisk. "We'll wait for daylight, then walk it if you're able. Bearers won't go down Crookspine Stair."

A few hours later, Moabet saw why. Dalu had gone beforehand to prepare for their arrival. She and Stilpin moved through littered alleys, unpeopled except for sleeping beggars and stuporous drunks, to the no-man's-land of a sunlit, utterly deserted square.

"Shandar territory from here on," he said.

It seemed at first that they must dwell in the sky. On one side of the square, a gateway framed airy blue and one thin cloud. When she stood beside him under the arch, Stilpin pointed down. A wedge of shadow slanted down where a narrow valley split Xalycis Rock. The shadow stopped abruptly along one rock face. The rest of Ladder Valley blazed with color—a jumble of painted houses receding until light and shadow met deep below. Thin sounds rose along with blue threads of smoke.

One hundred, two hundred, three hundred steps down the switchback stairs. And the cliffs became outcroppings of houses.

Houses gaudy as parrots: azure, scarlet, viridian, decorated with pinwheels, sunbursts, arrowpoints, flames, plaster and stone mimicking the bright wooden wagons that once traveled the plains of Shand. It was a nomad encampment thrust permanently into place, clinging like a transplanted vine. On rooftops and rope ladders children swarmed, masked for a festival. Paper faces of dogs and demons, heroes and gods, bobbed above small naked bodies, pausing now and then to inspect the newcomers. Shrill cries echoed from the cliffs.

An older boy came to meet them. Solemn amid the hilarity, he conducted them along a trail that cut across flat roofs, angled down steep slopes, and finally reached a stretch of level ground occupied by a group of particularly impressive buildings. The place appeared to be besieged by musicians. They were camped around the outer walls in a riot of wailing reeds and thunderous drums.

"Good luck to practice here by Great-grandfather's house," the boy explained. "And they're greeting his return from Deadwall Town."

"Their name for the rest of Xalycis," Stilpin murmured in her ear.

"The gods are listening," the boy added confidently.

Stilpin wondered what they thought of the racket. The *dead* were probably awake and listening too.

A two-leaved gate broke the mural of stylized running horses, russet and gold on a field of incandescent green. A small child opened the gate at the boy's peremptory knock. Beyond lay a courtyard where adults moved purposefully while children raced in random zigzags.

A round-faced matron, one of Dalu's daughters, bustled up and took charge. Stilpin found himself relieved of the percept. As Moabet vanished somewhere in a maze of small rooms, he was recruited to organize an incoming load of foodstuffs; feeling like the lad who once ran errands at Vuorn House, he surrendered to these mad Shandar for the rest of the morning. At least she would be protected here. Robellac would have his hide if the percept came to harm.

When he returned to the Valley four days later, he found Moabet in Shandar tunic and leggings, her hair in an untidy plait. She had a large basket propped on her hip and stood talking to a strikingly handsome man. Where most Shandar had a thatch of dust-brown hair, his mane gleamed with golden highlights. He was shirtless, with a lean, muscled body. Why wasn't he helping her with that basket?

"Here, let me take that," Stilpin said. As he plucked it from her, his arms rose ludicrously, for it was quite empty.

"You'll be Stilpin, I expect." The Shandar had an impudent gleam in his uptilting, greenish eyes.

Stilpin remembered him then. A dancer by trade. Hadn't they once passed an evening flirting with the same woman at a Low City inn?

"Railu Knifedancer," the man declared. "Grand-nephew to Dalu Drum-priest. Will you stay for the rites and the feast tomorrow? It's one of our great days, the Sun Marriage." He didn't wait for an answer, but gave a nod to Moabet and sauntered away.

Moabet retrieved the basket. "He's a local celebrity, doing the god dance for his second year."

Stilpin shrugged abstractedly.

A trace of concern entered her expression. "Has anything—?"

"No, no change. Arnix held a gala last night and came through unscathed, I'm told. He doesn't act worried."

"Worrying wouldn't help him." She seemed certain that the murder would occur.

"What if it's weeks, or months, from now?"

"Well . . ." a sidelong glance. "I shall have to learn to play the finger drums and cook barley-and-onion stew, I suppose."

"Or I can get you a market stall, telling fortunes." He spoke more sharply than he had intended. It nettled him, the way she had taken to these Shandar.

She fixed her full stare on him then but made no reply.

Stilpin's apology died in his throat. He felt that flickering chill again, like a shadow across the sun. Defeated, he turned away without another word.

Ladder Valley lay deep in shadow, under a paling sky, when the compound stirred to life.

Dalu and an ancient woman presided over the ceremonial making of fire in the central courtyard. As the first sparks flared up, sunlight reached the jagged cliffhead far above. The crowd's hush gave way to a great cheer.

When firepots had been distributed, to relight ovens left cold all the previous day, a frenzy of cooking began. Soon the air was delirious with rich smells. Outside the compound, the musicians strove valiantly.

Then the revels commenced.

Ladder Valley's great meeting hall was filled to bursting with Shandar and food, food in astounding quantities—

baked, fried, and roasted meats, the ubiquitous barley-and-onion stew, honeyed fruits, lavish pastries, and rivers of beer. For the first hours, eating was praise enough to the gods of Shand.

The dancing started late in the afternoon. A file of old men and women formed between the ranks of tables and shuffled to the thump of a single drum. When the pace quickened they matched it, breathing easily, jewels swaying in their lengthened earlobes like pendulums marking time. Stilpin watched, tapping a foot, losing his place now and then as the rhythms grew more complex. The sudden wailing of a company of reed-players set a host of younger Shandar into motion.

At the head table beside Dalu and his wife, Railu Knifedancer clearly itched to join in. As raucous horns blared and two girls ran into the crowd with staffs wound with ribbons and bells, it was too much for him. He leapt into the revelry with a laugh.

"He'll be worn flat before the god dance," Stilpin commented.

Moabet shook her head. "As soon wear out the sea." The same might be said of every Shandar. Their capacity for food, drink, and stamping reels was astonishing.

Outside the open doors, the courtyard filled with twilight. Silhouetted, a young boy juggled breadrolls, chanting to himself, "Knife, knife, knife." In time the chant spread. Musicians took up the beat, till the room shook with it. The sound became rhythmic applause when Railu sprang onto a table, stripped off his full-sleeved festival shirt, and held out his arms. Ten knives flew into his grasp.

Ten knives, spinning in the torchlight to a whirl of wild music: arcs of reflected flame around the dancer, concealing, revealing movements of uncanny grace. It looked so easy, natural as breathing, but Stilpin had heard the blades were steel "so sharp they'd cut a sigh." They flashed a hairbreadth from Railu's arms, slipped over his back like a cloak, returned leaping to his hand. At the climax, explosive acrobatics. Sweat sprayed from the dancer's whipping hair as he cartwheeled through a dizzying spiral of knives.

The knifedance brought an end to the general feasting. Diehards huddled over the last morsels or sought out dwindling supplies of beer, but most of the crowd simply relaxed on the long benches or wandered at random, greeting friends.

Beyond the circles of torchlight, mysterious preparations were under way amid whispering and muted laughter. By imperceptible degrees, in the course of the next hour all the great room grew quiet. At last one sound emerged: the slow pulsing of a drum. As the torches were doused, a subtler glow was revealed: coals in claw-footed braziers, half veiled by slow coils of smoke. The smoke had a feral reek. Stilpin looked back sharply and swore under his breath.

For a long time nothing happened. Drumbeat, smoke, a room of quiet people. Then the drum broke into stealthy pattering and a figure crept through the shadows. Man-beast: human body with a horse's massive head, mane cascading heavy and black. A wild thing stepping warily, alone under night sky, it would flee at a shift in the wind. The heavy head swung from side to side, then lifted. Among the dim, clustered stars a light was growing—a mote, a spark, a sudden blaze. Thunder! The creature sprang high as if flung into the sky, hung a long moment, then plummeted, to leap again as soon as heels struck ground. And again. Whirling now, mane hissing across muscled shoulders, he rode a tumbling flood of light: Lady Sun, drawn into being by a nightwish, desired, desiring, a devouring fire. Goddess.

Horse Man danced, a blur in the brightness. Gate and axletree, goddess and god, spinning and still, they were storm in a cloudless sky.

Stilpin's heartbeat raced, and he felt a moment's vertigo. Closing his eyes, he was falling. . . .

Moabet gazed to the limits of vision, fires ringing the horizon in a flickering wall, scarcely visible, and beyond them vague forms, moving in slow reflection of the god dance. Almost she could see—a figure drifting backward (falling?), a cluster of weird horned beasts (or men?), and a second, shadowy dancer following a rhythm of his own, apart from sun and thunder and sky. There was frost in the air, under summer stars.

The Shandar rejoiced, in the plains of their hearts' home, as the covenant of their people was affirmed once more, in abiding power. The Long Cold was past, and Lady Sun would walk in their paths till the world's end.

Thunder. Hoofbeats. Hands upon a drum. Dalu Drum-priest brought the dancer back from his journey.

What had been Horse Man became Railu Knifedancer, chest heaving, mouth agape with exhaustion. The mask lay beside him like a severed head.

For Moabet the journey had not ended. Still the flames rose far ahead, in constant, restless motion, and the forms beyond beckoned.

"Moabet! Sera Shar!" Who was calling her from her dream? For a moment her vision blurred, doubled. A face looked into hers with the fire ghostly in its flesh. So familiar, she knew it as she knew herself. . . .

She was seeing him now, Stilpin was sure of it, but her expression was so strange, half smiling, intimate. "Can you hear me? Come, take my arm. We'll walk."

The Shandar moved aside so they might pass—a few gave indulgent smiles to the outsiders and wished them good loving in the gods' sweet night. Stilpin nodded, with an inward curse for their low minds and their damnable witchfires. When the crowd was behind him, his furious anxiety began to subside. She was still on her feet, not like at Arnix House, and (gods be thanked!) she'd kept quiet this time. Was this some different kind of trance? The festival's cheerful uproar was far enough now that he could hear his feet crunching on the dirt path. Overhead the stars blazed, scattered thickly as in the vision of the god dance. The night air was cool.

"Breathe it in, deep. Get that poison out of you."

"Poison?" She blinked and drew a little away from him.

"They were burning it on the coals. An active essence, maybe two. Vuorn taught me enough to guess— Damn that bastard Dalu!" he exploded. "Why didn't he warn me?"

"Active essences." Moabet examined the idea. "Something like perfume essences, but stronger. Illicit?"

"Yes. For a chemic to abuse his knowledge so—"

"A drum-priest," she interrupted. "Who do you think discovered that essence? Bored grandees in search of a thrill? What we witnessed tonight was sacred, old as the Ice. A link between the people—a vow sworn and kept."

Her sudden vehemence surprised him. It was fierce as his own outrage had been. Now he felt only confusion. "Whatever it was you felt, it left me out. Was it anything like— but no, you didn't remember last time."

"That's just it!" she cried. "I'm conscious, I *remember* this. And I saw something—it might have been past, not future, but it was Vision." Her voice broke with the intensity of her thoughts. "Always before, I've wakened up to hear the others speak of wonders. They had nothing to do with me. I wasn't there. Do you see? This was different. *Real*."

A percept's first experience of her own uncanny powers. Stilpin hunched his shoulders under the weight of the night, and the cruelty of the gods. Some of the smoke must still be lingering in his brain, for it seemed the stars were laughing.

* * *

The Arnix vaults stood open, door after door gaping wide on gold and amber, ivory and jade, a room of butterflies, a room of skystones. Nothing had been touched, it seemed, for how could these chambers have held more? Toss in a single gem, and the air might explode with raining treasures.

Arnix had always trusted the massive outer door better than his guards. He held the keys; they ventured in only in the wake of friends brought to view some new rarity. No one had seen all the collections together like this, not even Aubric's sons.

It had been a quiet night. It was a quiet morning, save for the clatter of the day-guards' boots and the flutter of flame in the lamps, intruding upon the darkness of the vaults. Door after door . . . the guards moved slowly, sensing what they would find at the last, while they prayed it would not be so.

As if a plain man's prayer could turn aside the spinning die cast by the gods. Hadn't Arnix himself been told how this throw would end?

The younger guard moaned. He could smell it now. With a curse, the other man raised his torch high and they surveyed the slaughter. Just one corpse, but blood enough for a battlefield, the young man thought, choking back nausea. The elder walked past him, lit the lamp, and gazed on what had been Aubric i-Arnix. "Wasn't any kid with a penknife did that."

Better to look past the horror on the floor. Sound brisk, competent. "Anything missing? From the room, I mean." Damnation! He was making a hash of this. When he stumbled over a fallen relict, he shrieked—and the thing shrieked back. He would have fled then if his partner hadn't grabbed his arm.

"Yeah." Just the slightest break in the voice. The fingers

gripped tighter. "Twenty thousand orrins' worth of bad luck went out that door. Think it walked out by itself?"

The Artifact. The young guard pulled away and stood trembling, eyes wide with terror. "What if it d-did? Kill him and c-clear out?"

"Then we're well quit of it," the elder muttered. "Well quit." He turned for the door. "Come on, boy. Time to give 'em the word. The goddamned waiting's over."

III

Gherifan Arnix

The family mourned with stunned decorum. Aubric i-Arnix was gone, a prop kicked out from under the world. Resentment, anger, admiration, lost their reason for being. Quiet descended on a sometimes turbulent clan.

On most of them, anyway. In a house filled with the ashen hues of mourning, Gherifan Arnix wore defiant green.

The new i-Arnix, Berec, lacked his father's fiery temper. Slow in his movements and his speech, he came to anger with the imperceptible shiftings and sudden, massive momentum of waterlogged earth sliding down a hill. No predicting the moment of catastrophe.

But Berec's younger brother was prodding the slope. "Why assume this mock humility? Bleached sackcloth of the most elegant cut!" A gesture toward Berec's impeccably austere robe. "Shufflings and discreet murmurings as though *he* might hear if we raised our voices—but still the smile behind the hand, a little flirting in the corners, all manner of things that would draw down the wrath of the Great Departed if he happened to glance back this way from his cozy spot in Paradise. . . ."

"Gherifan. These ravings become you no better than that absurd outfit."

"Absurd?" Gherifan feigned bewilderment. "Well, I grant you it's last year's cut"—he flourished one tight-wristed sleeve—"yet the color remains in favor. You can see it anywhere on Wallwalk."

"Not in a house of mourning." Berec's eyes were cold beneath their drooping lids. The set of his mouth might merely have indicated boredom.

Gherifan's version of the family face—better formed than some, oval, without drooping jowls or beetling brow—displayed a bland composure. In a different setting, he would seem quite unexceptionable, this young man with the sleepy brown eyes and silky brown hair.

But Berec i-Arnix knew otherwise. "Brother, if you can't comport yourself properly, I must ask you to leave."

"Leave?" Gherifan seemed much struck by the idea. "Out the door with only the clothes—the offending clothes—on my back, and a brotherly curse at my heels? Cut adrift, vagabond, off on the road to adventure? Berec! You do me a favor."

Near to its final plunge, the sodden earth of Berec's temper found itself balked by an obstacle. "What? I didn't say. . . . There's no question that you'll stay and behave like a dutiful son with his father newly dead—"

"Murdered," Gherifan corrected.

"As you insist on saying. *Murdered*. You will give this family no cause for further disgrace or dishonor."

"Was it disgraceful of Father not to arrange a better death? Ah, of course it was. Perhaps I do take after him . . . in my own way."

"Out!" roared Berec, furious at last. "All right, go! But take your miserable wardrobe with you—and those idiot dramas you keep trying to spew back from memory—and those ridiculous masks! Take them all, fill half a dozen palanquins if that's what it requires. Do some of the servants catch your fancy? Cronies? Lovers? Lead the whole lot of them away, and cleanse this house of every trace of you!" Purple-faced, bellowing with nearly the force of the great Aubric himself, Berec made an awesome sight.

Gherifan glanced him up and down, then gave a brief nod. "All right. But no pack train of baggage and no purge in the servants' hall. There's none will mope themselves to death over me. I'm quite easy to forget, brother."

"I wish you'd 'forgotten' to be born!"

"Ah. The curse. Traditional to the last." And with those words Gherifan made his exit.

Out in the hallway, he trembled with reaction, and his eyes had a swimming brilliance as he looked around him, perhaps for the last time. Then he adjusted the set of his fine green shirt, stood a little straighter, and walked down the hall with a cool grace.

A man committing suicide rarely wants to depart the world anonymous, unless he has no friends to grieve, no family to disgust.

Gherifan Arnix decided to throw a party. As for death— let that august visitor come or not, master of revels or absent guest. He had often wished his father dead. . . .

"Kill all the Arnix!" he cried experimentally, alone in his rented room. "Pitch the gilded bastards over the city walls!" Ludicrous overplaying. But he could imagine himself falling, tumbling so the sky flip-flopped and the sun wove a ribbon around him, while the angry voices floated down on his heels.

What was the use of an Arnix? A creature to enrich, envy, and hate. Father had played the part to perfection, knowing no better than to be himself.

Anything but that. Gherifan's thought had the force of a prayer. Once more he put himself in the mind of a rebel, ragged and furious on the ramparts of High Xalycis. "Damn the Arnix," he said aloud. And laughed. *By our very nature, we're already damned.*

"Gherifan's drunk."

"Drunk's not the word for it. He's drowned and that's his corpse keeping us company."

"Well, he *said* it was his own wake, and the hell with dear dead Father. Anyone got a clean sheet? Or a not so clean one—good enough for a drunkard's shroud. Strip him and wrap him up: a package for the gods!"

"Thergol, there's women present."

"Then we'll have help, won't we?"

When Railu Knifedancer made his belated entry to the Inn of the Dancing Dog he found Gherifan Arnix insecurely swathed in a length of old cotton, bare legs dangling from the table where he perched alone in the place of honor, cradling an enormous tankard. A roomful of Artists Vagabond —actors, acrobats, singers, even a trainer of dancing dogs —surged cheerfully and obliviously around him. Strange, that way he had of slipping out of thought when he didn't want your notice. Railu had known him long enough to wonder at it. Now the Shandar's handsome face drew into a grimace of impatience as he swept aside a group of welcoming friends and made his way toward his erstwhile host.

"Goddammit, Arnix, you'd make a trussed sow weep for pity of you."

"Not Arnix," Gherifan muttered vaguely. He gripped the tankard tighter and swayed.

Railu steadied him. "Why not?" Accepting a drink from a passing potboy, Railu kept his attention on Gherifan. Was he really as drunk as he looked?

"They're all ghosts up there. Those Arnix. Hell with 'em."

"They're family. Lousy Shandar you'd make." Railu cleared away a litter of cups and sat next to Gherifan. At least they'd left him his rings. Though the rest of the gear would turn up in the morning—Gherifan was well enough liked, for all he was a grandee's son. That runaway summer with the players, he'd done all right.

"Can't be a Shandar. Born on Wallwalk."

"Well, you claim you're not an Arnix anymore, so why not?"

"You said I wasn't . . . that I was 'lousy Shandar.' Right! Your own words."

"I'll tell you what one of us'd do if someone—head of the clan, like Dalu—got himself murdered. We'd be wild for vengeance."

"Don't know who did it."

"Hell, that never stopped anyone in the tales. They'd have ghosts on the bedpost with blood pouring from their mouths—naming names too, you understand—and horses looking up from their feedbags to tell the hero where he's supposed to go."

"That's tales, strawbrain."

Railu flicked a glance at him. Half sober at least, to get that out in one try. But would he listen to anything but nonsense?

"So then, Gherifan No-name. No vengeance, if the horses won't talk. Come to Ladder Valley anyway."

Maybe he *was* blind drunk after all. Gherifan stared into nothing, with a weird smile. Railu took another swig of wine. Downright uncanny that smile was. "What the hell are you looking at? See a ghost after all?"

"No. . . ." Faraway voice—was he going to pass out? Then Gherifan declared, every word distinct, "But what *would* the horses say?"

Railu hadn't the slightest idea what he meant.

On the edge of the Tumbles, crude wineshops quaking with candlelight stood next to black alleys where dogs roamed and beggars slept in doorways. Rich men's palanquins came guarded and the lampmen went well armed, for dogs weren't the only waking things that moved in packs through Tumbleside. Danger spiced a visit to Masquer's Inn.

Massive torches burned by the gate in cylinders of glass, illuminating the strangest building in Xalycis. Five stories, all of reddish stone, it swarmed with faces: rough-hewn rogues leering beside blank-eyed dreamers, grave counselors clustered around drainspouts, windowsills overrun by a tide of forms, and balconies so intricately carved they looked like rotting lace. One high window shone with a pure, unblinking light. The master of the inn was in his aerie.

Beeswax candles flamed in sconces set all about Jabel Fivesides's private office. On his desk of polished wood with fittings of crystal and brass, a network of thin scars caught the light. A duller sheen silvered Jabel's close-cropped hair as he bent over the desk. Arm steady, muscles working in the wrist, he cast the pair of five-sided dice that had brought him his name and his fortune. They clicked, spun on their points, and tumbled to a rest. Like the last dozen casts, their sum was seven. When he felt the luck running in him, he could throw sevens all night. Jabel no longer looked to see how the dice landed. He was deep in thought.

The master of Masquer's Inn noticed things that other men missed: the violence behind a genial smile, the racing heart of a gamester feigning boredom, the seeds of beauty in a scrawny young whore. And now the talents of the inn's newest hireling, Leandric Gath. A swaggerer's name, but the lad didn't swagger. He had a sharp, wary look, yet Jabel had seen him in the Kennels defusing a brawl with a few easy words. Lowtown toughs absently called him "mate," and Wallwalk swells accepted wine from him with the nod they'd give a comrade. Whatever passions he might harbor, Leandric Gath kept a lid on them. Dangerous? Maybe. But useful? Oh yes, Jabel had uses for a man like Gath. Wait with your eyes open, and anything you want will come to your hand.

The dice chattered, stilled, flew again. Sevens, the number of luck.

Gath rose from scullion to upstairs servant in the course of a week, then found himself proposed for the ranks of "leaners" under the rule of Jabel's henchman, Iron Mog.

For his interview with Mog, he was led into a room of fiery carpets, heavy furniture, and walls ranked with weapons and trophies of the hunt: a powerful room, overwhelmed by its occupant.

Mog wore wristlets big around as a slave's collar. His features displayed less feeling than the stones of Masquer's Inn. No one met him without fear.

"Gath." The voice was a low rumbling, as much felt as heard. "Fivesides has a notion you could go the leaner's run, never mind you're short on muscle." A comprehensive glance stripped Gath bare. "Not a game for yessir, nosir potboys with ambitions. Had a boy come back less three fingers once, and he was lucky."

"I'm fair with a knife, and I don't stop thinking when there's blood on the ground," Gath answered with a direct look. Not everyone cared to meet Mog's yellow eyes.

With a week's experience in the Inn's brand of Low City cant, Gath had mentally translated the offer. To go out as a debt collector—a dangerous job it might be, but Jabel Fivesides thought him up to it. He had come to trust in Fivesides's instincts. "Straight fee or part-share?" he asked.

"More you bring in, more you get." Mog's impassive gaze moved unchanging from Gath to a burnished spear in the wall rack behind him, and on toward the window. After that first, raking stare, his eyes seemed to pass right over the young man who stood before him. He spoke to some midpoint in the air. "Tell you the drill. You read names, numbers?" Most Xalycans could manage that much with the aid of a clumsy finger and a frown.

Gath nodded.

"Leaners get a list," Mog continued. "Some jobs, the joker takes finding. Then there's times you walk right in. You get a feel for it or you don't last."

A one-shouldered Low City shrug. "Sounds all right."

Bold enough words from a lad of twenty-odd, a half-grown beard stubbling his oval face. Could be Jabel was right again. Gath was no coward—and no lackwit, for all the lazy droop of his brown eyes.

"You'll start tomorrow morning. Go to Pike, he'll set you up."

A nod from Gath, and it was done.

So, by a name invented in jest and once used by a runaway boy, the second son of Aubric i-Arnix became a debt collector in the service of Iron Mog.

Some leaners specialized in the defenseless. No matter if they were short on orrins, they could pay with household goods or the persons of their sons and daughters. Gherifan/Gath set his sights on the elusive and the stubborn. In his first days, he survived a clumsy knife thrust, a footrace through stinking alleys, and a half-successful seduction by a seasoned whore. As he gained experience, he had fewer adventures and better profits. Shabby Leandric Gath invested in finer clothing and paid for his barbering. He went after the merchant class most often now: hard-eyed shopmen with a taste for gaming and little luck, latecomer relict dealers who'd dreamed too high and borrowed too deep, a few jokers with their wealth intact and tight fists.

To the other leaners, Gath's successes began to smell of witchery. They called him Honeytongue, with much coarse joking, but few sought his company for a drink or a bout of dicing.

His aptitude disturbed Gherifan himself. People opened their lives to him so readily. But wasn't that what he was after, prowling the Low City like a spy? Somewhere within the wild speculations, feverish talk of magic on the loose and cults run mad, there must be a moment's cold truth—and a murderer's name.

Pike returned sullenly one night, cursing "that goddam bitch in her goddam fortress."

"Been to see the Widow, hey?" a companion grinned. "Hell, why do we try? Honeytongue's here to do the job for us, isn't he?"

Pike had worked on the Widow with a stubbornness nearly matching her own. But her entry-proof house and her legalist nephew who clerked for the Vinculine gave her too much of an advantage. She had no young children to hold hostage, no secrets to nose out for a threat of blackmail. Her late husband's gaming debt remained unpaid.

"Go on, let Honey slip it to her." The first in a chorus of suggestions, each lewder than the last.

Finally Pike cracked a smile and turned to Gherifan. "Well, Gath Honeytongue, how's your luck with widows?"

Gherifan's fingers played with his belt buckle. He uttered one of his rare jokes, of an inventive obscenity guaranteed to win the leaners' noisy approval. The room rocked.

When he came to the end of a long wheeze of laughter, Pike took the master list and ringed the entry with a wine-stained finger. Dramis Murn, the glass collector's widow.

Leandric Gath in Low City mourning presented a somber sight. Breeches and coat the color of crow wings, grief-scarf wrapped into a helmet shape framing a pale, still face, he stood at Dramis Murn's gate like an epitome of loss, and thought, *Berec i-Arnix, if you could see me now!* An inscribed card projected from ink-stained fingers toward the grillwork where a suspicious manservant confronted him.

The Widow Murn liked to conduct her own confrontations. A stately figure in mourning as severe as Leandric's own, she advanced toward the gate with a measured tread. "What is it, Parre?"

"He said he wanted to see you. Tried to give me his card."

"Permit me." Coolly she took the card that the visitor still extended. "You are Leandric Gath, scribe, of this city?"

"I am, Sera Murn."

"What is your business here?"

"Some of us—scribes, clerks, merchants," he began earnestly, "are joining together in a committee aimed at the rising violence in Xalycis. Theft, unprovoked attacks, killings, they are becoming intolerable. Criminals thrive, and the Guard does nothing. If this goes on, someday soon they may form an army against us. Already, their victims number in tens of tens." Impetuously, his eyes met hers. "They robbed and murdered my father. I understand that your husband was also murdered, here in his own home."

It was only a rumor around the markets and inns where the merchant Murn had been known, but Gherifan had seized upon it.

The Widow held his gaze for a long moment. "You've

suffered violence," she declared at last. "Whether you're a fool, a rogue, or an honest man, I'll grant you that. Come in, I'll tell you what happened here. Perhaps a committee of clerks can do more with the information than the Guard has."

Parre opened the gate with well-concealed amazement.

Beyond locks, bars, and gateman lay merchant opulence. Murn had not operated on the grand scale of a Jirmahad or a Robellac, but his business in rare spices brought an ample return. Enough for furnishings that would not disgrace a Wallwalk mansion, and enough to fund a passion better known now than the man himself. Glass collector Murn, follower of auctions, prowler of shops and bazaars, was a devotee of things transparent, translucent, pure or patterned, cloudy or bright, fragile—all of them fragile. Yet his home was not a storehouse jammed with the fruits of acquisitive decades, for Murn preferred to trade, always seeking a greater perfection. At the time of his death, he owned twenty-one masterpieces.

It surprised Gherifan that Murn had kept room in his mind for gambling or the other pleasures of Masquer's Inn. Perhaps the sight of his flawless glass and his elegant wife sometimes palled.

The Widow walked through her house without lingering over its fine appointments. She led her visitor straight to the back, where a heavy door opened onto an expanse of cool whiteness that startled the eye. A small room under an airy dome with a skylight at its center. Shelves and niches broke the curving line of the walls, while beneath the skylight stood a viewing pedestal of white marble. All were empty save the pedestal, where a tiny object shone intensely blue.

"My husband had this in his pocket, and the thief who killed him missed it." She picked it up and showed it to him. A miniature lion, exquisitely detailed down to the claws on its upraised paw, the muzzle wrinkled in a snarl revealing teeth like splinters of frost. The glass was brilliant as a sapphire. Gherifan had never seen a thing so beautiful, not among all his father's treasures.

"He must have suspected something at the last and hidden this," she went on. "Normally he wouldn't have dreamed of risking an object of this quality with such casual treatment. Somehow it survived—while he did not."

"How did it happen?" Gherifan asked in a low voice. "What manner of murder?"

"Much like the slaughter of a beast on the cutting block," she replied flatly.

A memory of splashed blood filled Gherifan's mind, vivid in the room's whiteness. He blinked, and it vanished. For a moment, he was too shaken to speak.

The Widow looked at him inquiringly. What images must her own memory present when she entered this room? She was strong, stronger than he.

"My father died so," he said. "The same slaughter, the —selective theft. The rest of your house was untouched? Yes. You have no idea who could have done this?"

Her thoughts had shifted, and for the first time she betrayed sadness. "Just before it . . . happened, we had spent such a delightful evening. It was my nephew's birthday, and our visitor—well, he did us great honor. A man of wit and judicious praise. My husband smiled as I'd rarely seen him. Proud, joyous." A pause, and the sadness returned in greater measure. "I find myself believing that the gods begrudge us our joy. Folly, would you say?"

"Power, pleasure. They seem jealous of their every prerogative," he answered bitterly. "They will leave us with nothing." He might have been talking of Aubric i-Arnix's death—or of his life, as master of his sons.

"Young man." She extended the hand still holding the glass lion. "Take this. Support your cause or yourself with it, I don't care what you do so long as you take it from this house. Keep it if you wish. I'll give you money as well. Try to find the killer—give me your word."

He gave it unreservedly.

Then the lion lay in his palm, casting a clear blue shadow. "You do me too much honor, Sera Murn."

"Probably so, Leandric Gath, but you do me a service all the same. Come, I'll have the piece wrapped for you. Murn would wish it." She turned away and walked to the door. "Treat it gently."

Gherifan stared down at the gift of blue fire. A potent talisman—that would shatter in the grip of an ungentle hand.

"What do your leaners think of him, Mog?"

"They've come round to him. Funny kind of leaning, though."

"He's a diplomat," Jabel grinned. "Go on."

"Changes his look depending where he's gone, they say. Doesn't go much for flash." In Mog's expressionless rumble, the description was neither blame nor praise.

"He will, if he makes it through." Pensive now, Jabel rubbed his long, clean-shaven jaw.

"Through what?"

"I have in mind a hawking," the innmaster declared with a Hightown drawl.

A grunt from Mog.

"Think he won't fly? I'll lay you odds."

"Hawking. Hasn't been here long, for you to call a hawking." Mog's cold, blank stare lingered for a moment on Jabel. "No bets. You're riding your luck."

"Maybe."

A pause. "Let me set him up."

Jabel considered, stroking his jaw again. "Don't rip his guts out, Mog. Right? I want the test, not just the setup."

"He'll be hawked proper. I'll see to it."

Within the hour, word went round Masquer's Inn. *Hawking*—it hung in the air like the stink of violence. Some men shivered. Others smiled.

Gherifan got the news in the usual manner, as a hasty warning. On his way back to the inn after a job, he found Pike walking next to him, speaking in a rapid whisper. What Pike said made Gherifan slow, legs suddenly wooden. Hawking. A test with a big payoff. All Jabel's top men had "flown." Fail, though, and he might join the crippled beggar at Jabel's gate—old Hawk, with his crazy, hating stare.

"Show heels now, you'd be right and tight. Just don't come back." Pike's hoarse whisper vibrated in his ear. "If you're still game, it's for now. No waiting. Luck, Gath."

Gherifan watched Pike's leather-clad back receding and vanishing down the crowded street. "Show heels now"—he could do it, cast off Leandric Gath in minutes, probably make his peace with Berec and be back on Wallwalk, set for life. What kind of life, though? He thought of the Widow Murn with her silent house and the bare white treasure room.

He began to walk again, toward Masquer's Inn.

An oddly ceremonial beginning—the black hood, the rope tied around the candidate's wrists in silence, no crude joking. Barefoot, sightless, he could have been proceeding into a shrine of the Triune God for a night of vigil. But the silence beyond the door was charged with expectation. A roomful of men waited to unleash bedlam. Was Jabel there? No telling.

"Leandric Gath." Iron Mog's deep voice froze the breath in Gherifan's lungs. "You know the drill. It starts here."

With no more prologue, Mog's mallet fist struck his shoulder hard enough to break the skin. Another pair of hands steadied him. Blows to the stomach, the head, and already there was pain, blood, shame, for he knew he'd scream the next time. He was screaming now—but the watchers' yells engulfed his cries. How long before bones, bowels, flesh dissolved under that onslaught? When he jerked up his bound hands, involuntarily, agony flashed from a broken finger. Eyes flooded, nose swollen like a snuffling boy's, Gherifan gulped in breaths through the damp fabric of the hood, deaf with the endless noise, stunned by endless pain.

But the end came—for a while.

It looked like a corpse, dumped in the ravine by furtive men. A very fresh corpse, still bleeding, bruises rising black. Evening light fell serenely on the scene. A light breeze rattled through the weeds and dry brush of Hawk Run. Oddly for such a violent beating as the body had received, the face remained almost unmarked, peaceful.

The eyes opened.

Grasses moved before him, a shadowy blur that brought on nausea. He doubled over, retching into the weeds. Slowly the world ceased to tilt and plunge. Gherifan squinted toward the sky, where a few stars shone cold and still. Cliff's edge silhouetted black. Hawk Run.

With a grunt of pain, he levered himself up and stood, swaying. Dried blood, piss, dirt. *You stink, Gath. Get moving, find the water.*

Gherifan knew Hawk Run. It split two great estates on Wallwalk, a jagged gash in the cliffs. A boy might slip away from his tutors and come down here to watch the hawks and dream, or splash in the rock pool. Was it still there? He stumbled toward the right-hand slope, where runoff from the Demedrin gardens collected in a natural basin. A gleam of reflected sky. Yes.

He bent down and drank. Washed himself, shivering. Then went back for the hood they had tossed down beside him when they left him there, naked. With a piece of jagged rock, he managed to open it at the seam. He tore off a thin strip. It would do for his throbbing finger, if he could knot it tight without passing out. And the rest would make a slave's loin-clout. Appropriate.

Mog had been here once. Maybe Jabel himself. They would have gone down, following the ravine to where it narrowed and became a trash dump for an obscure section of the Middle City. Not far to Tumbleside from there, he supposed, if you knew the way. So, back to the inn with nothing to face but a gauntlet of Jabel's men, on the lookout for a staggering hawksman. Mog had faced them straight on, he'd heard the story. Just walked buck naked into the inn, and only one poor fool dared get in his way. Mog, Bek, and the others had gone down Hawk Run. But Gherifan would go up.

At Masquer's Inn, midway through the night, an unusual number of guards lounged at the doors, in all states from drunkenness to irritable alertness. Deadline for new bets had passed, and stories of old hawkings had grown stale. Had Gath died up on the Run, or maybe just slunk away? But lampmen and guests were still arriving, and a few beggars moved in the shadows. He could be out there, about to try to bluff or fight his way in to Jabel Fivesides. Odds were, he'd aim to sneak in while some drunken fool ranted and drew all eyes. But they were ready for that. Crude clubs hidden under half-closed jackets. A few sharp knives close at hand. Jabel might have a long wait for his boy to stroll back in.

The biggest palanquin of the night loomed up in the torch-light, an old-fashioned box on poles carried by two liveried men. Some Wallwalk ancient couldn't sleep, fancied his luck. Aye, an old one all right.

The grandee who emerged was hunched under a long bro-cade cloak, head wrapped in the kind of turban that had been the rage three generations back. Bloodshot eyes glared out at the encroaching beggars with icy contempt. They scuttled back to their places.

"Don't wait for me," he barked at the palanquin bearers. His lampman must have already melted away, no sign of him. Hell of a job, working for an old bastard like that.

Only one surprised beggar saw the grandee tip his bearers a wink before they hoisted the empty box and plodded back the way they had come.

Tight-fist. Not a penny for alms, nothing for the doormen or the coat-keeper—to whom he'd curtly refused to give up his cloak. Well, Jabel'd loosen those purse strings.

While the watchers mused on the comeuppance due to misers who go gambling, their attention had already shifted back to the street. Not one of them noticed that the grandee's feet were bare.

Getting himself up the stairs at a walk was worse than running up with a loaded tray. Gherifan was shaking with exhaustion. But his triumphant piece of trickery still delighted him, for all was fair in a hawking—even help from one's former servants. No matter if Iron Mog waited before Jabel's door, murder in his eyes. It had been worth it, to get this far.

No one waited in the corridor. Gherifan pulled himself a little straighter, assumed a sneer of arrogant ill-humor, and knocked with his good hand. "Innmaster! A word with you."

Jabel opened the door and frowned in annoyance at the elderly stranger with the grievance. Of all the times, it had to be . . . hawking night. He blinked. "Son of a bitch. Gath. You look like hell." And began to laugh, in great gusts that finally brought men racing up the stairs to see the innmaster ushering Gath (borrowed headcloth stripped from his haggard, grinning face) into the office to claim the winner's cup of wine.

* * *

The young heal quickly. Gherifan was already growing edgy from enforced idleness when the word came down from Jabel: Go see Bek. Another of Jabel's lieutenants, busy with some mysterious project for the last month. Gherifan had only met him once. What could the man want with him?

On a hot, bright afternoon, soldierly Bek rode beside Gath in an anonymous palanquin making the long climb to Wallwalk. Gherifan wondered if this were some obscure joke of Jabel's—revenge for his returning from the hawking in such style? Bek would tell him little, though Gherifan kept prodding.

"Guardpost ahead. You can get into this place with enough palm-grease?"

Bek pulled a slip of parchment from his tunic. "Not needed."

Gherifan felt a chill then. Maybe Jabel had found him out and was dumping him back at Arnix House in ignominy. He fell silent, staring at the passing scene.

But they went beyond the turning for Arnix House and on to a less fashionable part of the Walk, where houses and fortunes were newer, servants' livery gaudier. (Those bearers who'd brought him down in his great-grandfather's ridiculous old palanquin, they'd keep his secret without a bribe, but he'd find a way to get money to them.) What was Bek saying?

"Enough gawping, lad. We're here."

They emerged before a sprawl of a house that had a look of recent desertion. Vines trailed brown across the outer walls, and weeds had sprouted from cracks in the front steps. Gherifan thought of a rumor he'd heard months ago, of a plunger on the western Walk, gone bankrupt.

"Big place," he remarked. "Who lives here?"

"Used to be a family called Nerra."

Nerra, that was it! Some relative of Vuorn's disastrous

wife. Born for scandal, that family. . . . Gherifan grinned to catch himself thinking like a proper Arnix. It was a little late for that.

Bek had unlocked the door with a massive key. Dust motes flew thick in the shafts of light slanting through the entrance hall. Footsteps echoed with no carpet to dull the sound.

"What're we doing here anyway? Place's already picked clean."

No answer from Bek. He led the way up a broad staircase to a level where there were signs of life. Less dust, for a start, then dropcloths on the floor. At the back of a long corridor, a single door had been newly varnished, scarlet and black. Bek opened it, to reveal a room of breathtaking gaudiness.

Gods, Knifedancer would love it!

Leandric Gath gave an awed whistle. "How much'd this cost? Who's it for? Jabel's new townhouse or something?" He grinned at the joke.

Bek ran a blunt hand down a wall hanging of crimson, purple, and gold, a design of angular, interlocked dragons. "It's for a westerner, name of Rodion." He turned back to look at Gath, a trace of amusement in the lean, bearded face. "He'll feel right at home here. And the marks'll love it."

"He's fronting a whorehouse? Hell, the place is too big."

"Not a plain whorehouse, Gath. An inn, with all the trimmings. Posh, exotic." He seemed to be quoting Jabel.

No need for pretense. Gherifan was honestly startled and impressed by Fivesides's bold venture, setting up an inn on the Walk. "Gods 'n' powers, the orrins will roll in." He looked around him again. "So, where's this westerner?"

Bek's hand clamped firmly on Leandric Gath's shoulder. "Right here." He propelled Gath to a wardrobe whose doors swung open on a riot of color. "All yours—Rodion."

Whooping, dizzy with the mad turn of fate that was sending

him back to Wallwalk, Gherifan plunged in, pulling out tunics, robes, glittering scarves, high, dyed boots. In short order he was decked in ruby red brocade, supple breeches so tight they seemed painted on, and boots to the thighs. Gilt tassels danced with each step. He eyed himself in a mirror of polished bronze. At least no one would ever recognize him in this gear. He scarcely recognized himself. Standing superbly poised, head high—if he slouched, he'd look a complete fool—Rodion the westerner gazed back from the mirror in barbaric magnificence. From nowhere came a thought: *A trap to catch a thief.* "We'll call it the Blue Lion."

"What? The inn?" Bek shrugged. "Fine by me, if Jabel goes for it."

A cooler, more definite statement. "It will be the Blue Lion." Then the pose broke and Gath ran a hand through his hair. "Hell, what's the accent? I'll need help setting this up."

"You'll have it, man. Don't you know? You're Fivesides's golden boy, he wouldn't trade you for a living mage with the secret of immortality in his back pocket."

Then Jabel Fivesides was mad as a ranting street-corner prophet, and would likely lose his shirt on this deal. But gods—what a lark!

IV

Perfume and Bones

Back on Wallwalk. Madness! How had she talked him into it?

Stilpin sat in Etroren i-Vuorn's formal parlor like a man awaiting execution.

Never trust the quiet ones. They can twist you around their finger with a few choice words. Of course it was Dalu's fault, playing with active essences as though centuries' use made it right.

Stilpin sighed, looking down at his boots. Moabet had become fascinated with chemicrye, essences, the perfume art. Hell, she was as bad as the mob that smashed up two odd-shops and a scent stall in the Market, crying "Mage-work!" Mage-work it was, she claimed, survivals of the lore Xalycis had so gladly cast off when its sorcerous rulers fell. Sister arts to the making of the Artifact itself.

He did not want to believe in magic. Minor perfumers crafted scents, and great ones made portraits. Chemics grubbed in the raw materials to produce essences. Only Tum-

bleside villains and mad Shandar drum-priests had the gall
to deal with actives.

He'd fallen into that one, so eager to get her away from
khur and knifedancers and trances, he happily babbled about
Vuorn, the perfume art . . . more essences.

Moabet Shar, perfumer's apprentice. Come on, Stil, stop
fretting—he's bound to turn her down. What did it matter,
if the interview in the library behind those closed doors had
gone on longer than expected? Vuorn was nervous around
women. He'd be slow, halting, achingly polite, couching
rejection in labored compliments. He'd—

The doors opened. Moabet was the first to emerge, smiling.
Then Vuorn, his pensive scholar's face unchanged, unreadable. Melancholy had settled on those features even before
his wife's desertion. Only the gray in the pointed beard was
new.

"Ah, Stilpin. Forgive us for keeping you waiting such a
time."

Us? Stilpin didn't like the sound of that. He mumbled some
mannerly nonsense in reply, and took a closer look at the
percept. Not just smiling—delighted. His heart began to thud
unpleasantly. But surely Vuorn's chemic would never agree
to help train her. Dalu had evaded her in Ladder Valley,
claiming priesthood as a male prerogative, a brotherhood of
khur and secrets.

A woman 'prentice in Vuorn House? Impossible.

Moabet could hold back no longer. "Stilpin, he's taken
me on!"

He turned his back on her and crossed to a window overlooking Vuorn's gardens. "Come here," he commanded.
"What do you see out there, Moabet, over the treetops?"

She joined him, as the perfume master trailed behind.
Above the trees rose an arrogant roof-peak, gleaming in the
sun.

"Arnix House," she said.

"Perhaps you've forgotten our little run-in with the Arnix. Or has Ladder Valley knocked all the caution out of you?"

"Stilpin—" Vuorn began.

"Ser?" Turning, he leveled a stare at his former employer. "Has she told you the trouble she's in?"

"I am aware of the prophecy, and its fulfillment. Terrible business. But you know me, Stilpin." A wan smile. "The Art comes before all else. Sera Shar has the aptitude to distinguish between the Nine Scents of Ice. She could remember and repeat the Fifty Noble Essences on first hearing."

Well of course she can, damnit, she's a percept! Stilpin swallowed the response. "Master. If the Helm find her here, you'll be seen as an accomplice. What work can you produce, shackled in a cell? The *least* penalty for a crime of blood is the loss of a hand."

Vuorn's hands were elegant, long-fingered, free of a chemic's stains. Born to wield a scent wand. They trembled slightly as the perfumer answered: "I shall do everything in my power to avoid the Helm's attentions. The very unlikelihood of Sera Shar's coming here gives us a degree of safety, I believe."

"But Ladder Valley—"

"Stewpots, dancing, and maybe a brood of pretty green-eyed children. What *work* would I have there?" Moabet demanded, with a passion that brought color to her cheeks as she flung his question back at him.

The sensible thing would be to offer to help her leave the city in secret, try to convince her she could find another Robellac to take her on and trust her with more than a scribe's duties. Stilpin did not have the stomach for that bland assurance. "Do as you like," he muttered.

"My clerk can make the arrangements." Vuorn gave a vague gesture. "Contracts, fees, what have you. You'll find him in the usual place."

Arrogant as old Arnix, however different they might seem. Grandees! Stilpin bent in an elaborate bow that concealed his spasm of anger. When he rose again, he was expressionless. "As you will, m'ser."

"Stilpin—" The percept looked back at him. Ready to explain, justify, bedazzle, delude?

"Good day to you, Sera Shar." With a curt nod, he turned and walked away.

Early the next morning Etroren i-Vuorn strode through his workrooms, humming under his breath. As always, discordances caught his eye—the empty jar of sea essence still awaiting replacement, the shelf of botched mixtures and distillations left by his last apprentice (poor fool, he couldn't tell rose water from camphor)—but the master perfumer's mood continued blithe. He paused at a table where vials of liquid essences sat neatly ranked, chose three of them not quite at random, stowed them in the padded case with the sheaf of crystal rods, and thrust the case back into his sash. Then he headed for the smaller of his perfume chambers.

Cinnamon, brick dust, black char. They would do for today's triad. He should have finished this weeks ago, testing the air flow at different dilutions, with the new fans.

The chamber was dim and pleasantly cool. Concealed mirrors angled narrow beams of light onto the central platform where the table stood like a performer in repose, tall on its three tapering legs.

"Portrait of a table," Vuorn murmured. "What essences express its soul?" He gave a soft laugh that echoed from the dome above him. Hadn't his own master posed problems almost as abstruse?

"Today you will endeavor to portray . . ." What had it been? Yes! "A lampman and a sparrow." Well-bred Wallwalk boys though they were, the students had laughed.

Setting out the different dilutions, with the air in the chamber utterly still, Vuorn recalled chemicrye three decades old. He smiled at the memory of the prank made famous as Gabbin's Stench, then sobered at the thought of the master's exquisite portrait of his daughter: leaves in the wind and distant flowers, with an undertone none of them could identify—the scent of loss, perhaps; the girl took ill and died within the year. She had worked alongside her father. Rarest of things, a woman perfume artist. Yet why not? Vuorn drew out three scent wands, splayed them, and dipped them into the first dilutions. Carefully he released the triad of essences into the swooping breeze called forth by his other hand on the ropes governing the fans. He always felt a trifle absurd, playing artist and performer at the same time, with his hair ruffling and his arms all akilter. Not a dignified picture. Then he set both memories and self-consciousness aside, for the essences had expanded through the chamber. In the way of a minor triad, they blended completely, no angular complexities intruding. Again Vuorn worked the fans. The triad was swept away on cool currents of air. Good. At that strength, sometimes essences lingered.

Now, the ideal dilution. Ah, yes. Scent of the city, this was—cinnamon, brick dust, char, you could smell it on the skin, it shaped the very forms of wit and resonated in a woman's smile. Moabet Shar had caught its quality as she took all things, deftly from the world around her, but it rested on the surface like a fine dusting of sand. Only in a woman Xalycis-born would the city's essence deepen and become the very ground-base of her soul.

As it had in Jesimis. Even as it slipped into his mind, Vuorn dismissed the thought, making himself busy with the ropes, the wands, the next dilution. The chamber must be fully readied by tomorrow, when Moabet Shar faced her first real test. He had no doubts of her success.

* * *

After Vuorn's courtly politeness in the morning's first session, his chemic was refreshingly blunt. "Take that jar of *airriz* crystals and grind them. Don't put more than two pieces in the mill at a time, or it'll seize up. Keep going till you're done. Takes an hour or so. And never mind asking me questions, girl. That comes later."

Moabet opened the tall jar full of grayish crystalline lumps, and a faint metallic odor drifted out. Ground to powder, the *airriz* would release a bitter reek.

"Here, you'd better have this." Dalu handed her a plain scarf to cover mouth and nose. "Your eyes may run a bit, but you won't poison yourself. When you're done, there's a bath through that door. Change of clothes on the shelf. There's no one clean as a chemic, no matter what some fools in the marketplace might say." He bent again over the huge mortar where a mass of fibrous black material had been yielding, slowly, to his powerful, rhythmic pounding. It smelled of rotting weeds, yet had a pleasant, elusive sweetness. An afterthought made him look up again. "The lads won't turn up their noses at you for the chemicrye. Not after a bath, anyway." And he gave her an impudent grin.

He received a cool stare in return, but the percept said nothing.

The Thirty-Three Perfect Essences, the Weather Scents, the Twelve Modes of Passion and the Four of Quiet Virtue, the Ladder of Beauty, the Sleeping Dragon—over the centuries, perfume masters had transformed their art from plain-spoken chemicrye to a strange and fantastical poetry/philosophy of sensuous abstractions. Still, it fell back into austerity when it came to notation. A portrait chart was a branching pattern of lines and symbols, stark as a winter tree.

Vuorn looked up from a chart spread out across a table as Moabet arrived for her afternoon instruction.

He sprang to his feet. "Here you are. Take a look at this—what do you think?"

A week ago she had never seen a chart. Today he challenged her with a vague, large question that would have daunted many second-year students of the art.

Moabet leaned to look. "The secondaries for the last of the Lesser Passions," she said almost immediately. "Saffron, alabaster, and the twelfth Fire scent. They make no sense." She did not hedge the response with qualifications, apologies, or questions angling for a hint of what the master might expect.

What must the life of a percept be, with such fierce, immediate comprehension at her command? Like living in the center of a fire, Vuorn thought, all swiftness and terrifying energy.

"The secondaries, yes," he echoed after a pause. "What would you suggest?"

"An error in notation. The alabaster should be something else—say, anise."

Vuorn unstoppered three vials in a rack on the table: saffron, Twelfth Fire, anise.

"I guessed it then!" Suddenly the percept gave way to the young woman, pleased and a little surprised.

He smiled. "Yes. Of course you did. Now, with the error resolved, tell me what personality this chart expresses."

And the lesson went on.

"Know how to build an Artifact yet?" Heavily ironic, Stilpin stood in the percept's open doorway. This had once been the room next to his own, tucked under Vuorn's attic. For a 'prentice's chamber, it looked unnaturally tidy, almost unlived in. But then, Moabet had no need for note-taking.

She sat cross-legged on her bed, severe in a plain brown dress, her hair bound back. "Vuorn's Art is fascinating of itself."

"Ah, you're taking a little holiday then. Worn out by work for Robellac, and play in Ladder Valley, the percept—"

"*You're* in a pleasant mood," she broke in.

"I'm ready to slaughter the world." He found a chair, drew it over toward the bed. "Item one: The Council finally passed the ban on further sale of relicts, but *grandees* may deal in what they already possess, provided they bypass lowly brokers like myself. Item two: The black market's firmly in Lowtown hands. Intrude, and lose some vital part of your anatomy. Item three: You predicted all this, I acted on your advice, and Robellac is filthy rich."

"So you're bored. The game's won and no one's willing to play with you now."

"I don't exist, as far as they're concerned! It's all Robellac's savvy, Robellac's fucking Luck." He became aware how petulant this sounded, and stopped, fists still clenched on his knees.

"Well, Ser Stilpin, what of a killer's luck? Any sign of the Artifact out there?"

"Not a thing. Someone's gloating, very privately."

"Or baffled by its wards."

His brows rose in inquiry.

"Do you leave a new-sharpened sword lying where a child can pick it up and play with it? The mages can't have been such fools. Yes, I know, they're gone," she forestalled his comment, "but I've heard no tales of brave, plain men wielding sorcerous objects against their makers. The mages destroyed themselves."

"So the Artifact's irrelevant, useless to the thief?"

She frowned. "I'd like to think so."

"Could someone like Vuorn get past these wards?" Stilpin

asked it in a low voice, as though some unfriendly ear might be pressed to the high window. His ill-humor was turning into uneasy nervous energy.

"Perhaps, given enough time."

"Could *you*?"

"Yes." No equivocation, just the one blunt word.

"Shit." He stared at her, gazed straight into the wide, unblinking eyes. *Not quite human* was his only thought in that moment. His mind emptied of calculations, plans, desires.

"I'm no mage, Stilpin, not even a back-alley witch." The bed creaked as she leaned forward and set a hand on his wrist. "If I survive this, maybe I'll set up as a second-rate perfumer somewhere."

He freed himself, held out a hand palm-up. "Pretend I've got a fortune in black *khur* and no scruples. What do you do?"

"Use you."

"Like you're using Vuorn, for purposes I'm too stupid to understand." His voice shook as he rose from the chair. "I'll leave you to it, percept."

Clerk Stilpin, coward and fool. The worst of it was, he knew that he'd come back.

She held the perfume wands delicately poised over the vials of essences. Vuorn signaled, and Moabet released the triad as he worked the fans.

So fixed on her task. If an audience sat in the tiered seats of the Greater Chamber and she stood on that broad stage, they would watch her as he did here, forgetting the portrait she performed. She was nothing like the woman of Vuorn's portrait, Margola with her cool, haunting beauty, her elegance that wakened into startling energy, then slept again. Margola, "Goddess of the First Dawn" one poet had called her, and the overblown phrase had not brought the usual jests from Wallwalk wits—for secretly, they shared his thought. To see her brought a kind of awe into the heart, a restless peace. . . .

And Vuorn recognized the paradox built into the portrait. Thinking all his attention rested on Moabet Shar, he had fallen once again into the essences' spell. Extraordinary how they overwhelmed even a personality as distinct as hers.

The final triad of wands set down, she was watching him, he suddenly realized, with an odd attention. Looking for what? Not a master's censure or praise. Why had she asked to perform this, his most famous portrait?

"The performer scarcely feels it—the power of it," she said as if in answer, though her voice held a question.

"Some do. They surrender to it, move in a kind of trance. Others say they feel nothing at all. But the audience is utterly caught up. You made me see that, just now. One moment you were there, the next my thoughts were all on Margola. Not admiring my own cleverness, mind you. Simply Margola herself."

"Then it's like a sort of mask, the portrait. Concealing me."

"A mask composed of many movements. More like a dance." That was how he had always thought of the art in performance.

She was gazing straight through him to something beyond, or within her mind. "Horse Man," she murmured. "Don't put it in the fire, *wear* it. . . ."

It was as well for Vuorn that these words meant nothing to him. Instead he fell to thinking about his apprentice's unreadable soul (was it merely difficult or quite impossible to capture in essences?), while she pondered a new conception of his art with a freedom that would have appalled him.

"A mask in motion," she said.

Lost in reverie, he did not hear.

* * *

Deliberately, Moabet worked herself into a state of exhaustion, spending the days with Vuorn and Dalu, the nights alone at a table littered with charts and notes. Her face became pale, sharp-boned, uncomfortably like a fox spirit in a folktale, or a woman with a demon lover.

In an access of guilt, Vuorn ordered his apprentice to leave off her lessons for a few days. Stilpin, more mistrustful, sought means to keep an eye on her, to oversee the percept's holiday. He imagined hours in Vuorn's gardens with a picnic under the trees, an evening's earnest conversation in a quiet room. But what he got was Tib.

Stilpin strode into the office above Robellac's warehouse on a bright morning, whistling, ten minutes' work to do and a day's leisure ahead. Even as he realized the door had not been locked, he spotted the urchin perched on his desk, booted legs swinging, hands in the pockets of an ill-fitting jacket. The pointed face split in an impudent grin. "Name's Tib."

He scanned the room wildly. No vandalism, no sign of theft. No large thugs lurking in dark corners. He grabbed the creature by its grubby collar. "What the—"

"Like the haircut?" it asked in Moabet's voice.

He felt a dangerous calm descend. "Have you ever been strangled? You've missed an interesting experience." His hands tightened fractionally around her throat. "Convenient of you to have trusted me this way."

"You know I trust you with my life."

As she spoke, voice vibrating under his palms, those falcon eyes faced him candidly.

"I should break your neck, percept." He thrust his hands into his pockets, in unconscious imitation of her pose. "You don't know how I'm tempted."

"Maybe I do." She crossed her legs, trim in borrowed breeches. Then deliberately changed the subject. "The second youngest kitchen boy's about my size. Loaned me his best suit of clothes for three coppers.''

He gave a hollow laugh. ''Very funny, Moabet. You certainly had me fooled. Now, shall we go home?''

''Oh, no, we're going to market. You and your new clerkling.''

Stilpin shut his eyes. Opened them. Tib was still there, rummaging in a pocket. Even the long lashes would not give the game away; plenty of boys had eyes the envy of a girl.

Tib pulled out a notebook, a bundle of pens, an ink pot, and a grubby bag of candy. ''I've got a slingshot somewhere in here, but I'll need some practice.''

''Are you out of your fucking *mind*?''

Sun poured down on the city. Dogs rolled, ecstatic in the dust, and beggars lounged. Waterboys, juice sellers, and dealers in cold beer seemed to multiply by magic, drawing crowds until their wares were gone. Stilpin unlaced his tunic, but his latest clerk (too strictly raised, or shy) followed him primly buttoned despite the warmth of the day. Neither agent nor clerk seemed to have an urgent errand as they wandered the markets on the fringe of the great bazaars. Out to enjoy the fine weather, no doubt, like half Xalycis.

They sucked the juice from sweet limes and wiped it away on their sleeves.

''Hey then, Tib. Where next?''

''What's that?'' Across the street, there was some bustle around a tradesman, and a flash of color in the strong light.

''Let's go and see.''

The peddler's would-be customers were fascinated but uncertain, poking each other and muttering, not quite meeting his eye.

''Gen-u-ine, straight from the Tumbles!'' he cried again. ''Moved by a mystical power, but small enough to fit in a child's hand—and priced for your pockets, ladies and gentlemen. See how the colors shift and shine!'' Though he never quite declared that his tray contained relicts, who would not think it? For the hues blazed, blurred, changed, now sharp as a rainbow prism, now soft as swirling oil.

"Master, can I have one, please?" Tib cried.

"Well now." Stilpin eyed the peddler. "How much do you want for one of those things?"

Brisk bargaining ensued. Finally Tib had his prize, wrapped in a scrap of leather, and master and clerk shared a grin as they went on their way.

"Haven't talked a man down like that in years," Stilpin declared with satisfaction. "Must've saved—what?—all of five coppers on the deal. Of course that bauble of yours is no relict. Sheer fakery."

"How was it faked, then? What materials did they use?"

"Brat. How should I know?" About to lift the cap and ruffle the cropped hair beneath, he stopped short. Then went and did it anyway, with a rather self-conscious manner. "So, Tib. Had enough for the day?"

"Aye, sir, if you wish. Thank you, sir."

Lightly, Stilpin cuffed the clerk's shoulder. "What a grateful little brat it is! Fair makes you sick to hear it."

Companionably, they began to retrace their steps.

"What do you think, Dalu?" Moabet, back in her women's clothes, face scrubbed, with a scarf hiding her short hair, still had a trace of Tib's pertness. "Did Stilpin waste three coppers?"

The chemic bent over the pseudo-relict, which now rested on a stone table under a good light. It was a twisted bit of metal that had flowed from heat, coated with a pigment that changed color in warm air but cooled to matte black. Held in the hand, it came to life again.

"I've never seen a pigment like this," he said. "Interesting stuff. I'd like to have more of it, find how it was made."

"Could it be the work of a chemic?"

"Has to be." He tugged one dangling earlobe. "Not a regular chemic, mind you. Low City peddler hawking the baubles for him like that, it'll be a renegade. Maybe a loner, maybe some boss man's maker." Dalu glanced up. "What are you after, haring with Stilpin into Lowtown? Vuorn thinks it's just a change of air, but I say you're out for mischief."

"It isn't the air—the *city*'s changing, and I want to see it. Whoever found the Artifact set enormous forces in motion." She gestured, an abrupt sweep of the hand. "Greed, envy, ambition, intellectual fascination, faith in its crudest form, and joyous delight in miracles. One object found, then lost again, and all that comes of it. That's the way the world moves on."

Dalu himself was fascinated. The percept's enthusiasm caught him up, and he forgot her doubts about her motives. During the rest of their talk she did not look once toward the mock-relict lying dormant on the table. The thought of a renegade chemic might never have engaged her mind for a moment. The percept's training stood her in good stead, closing like an iron shutter over thoughts that blazed into blue heat.

Even if Xalycis were not changing, it would have changed for Stilpin in the next days. He had moved on a narrow round between the formalized combat of the auction floor, the rough and tumble of more casual dealing, and the pleasures of tavern and bed. Now the pretty women seemed garish as painted statues, the taverns quick intervals of rest between adventures in that strange place he had never been before: Xalycis, seen through a percept's eyes.

He thought it was the new wealth of information that fascinated him. Tib, his brat of a clerk, asked impertinent questions, waited with unchildlike patience, and behold, the doors stood open! He heard tales of astonishing journeys made by simple porters, memories of old sorrows still strong enough to break the heart, explanations so lucid he felt he could pick up a man's tools and carry on the trade himself. It was heady as a sudden ability to read minds. The city became a torrent of voices, a trove rich enough for generations of poets.

But the voices were not all. He would pause for a moment to study the pattern of shadow on a sunlit wall, the sparkle roused in vacant air as the light passed through, the dance of radiance and mystery where Tib walked before him through bright, then dark. Stilpin came to know the special swing of that ill-fitting coat with its crammed pockets. Sometimes, Tib would turn and smile at him, a smile he had never received from Moabet Shar. Once when he pulled Tib back from the path of a runaway pushcart and its pursuing owner, the feel of flesh and tense muscle in his clerk's arm gave him an odd shock—more real, more vivid than the passing danger.

Alert to everything, yet walking in a dream, Stilpin provided an easy mark for the thin boy who had stalked him for the better part of an afternoon. Taddin Whistle drew the Santha's Hand from his outsize jacket (far shabbier than Tib's) and held it concealed beneath a dragging cuff. The familiar feel of thin membrane rippling with fluid pleased him. Drift closer now. . . . Yes!

In one explosive movement, Taddin hurled the sac. Blue dye burst over his quarry's clothes like huge handprints. The man was Marked, and the boy-clerk too where some of the dye had splashed wide. So be it. The Santha must mean to have them both.

The man swore in a rough, scared voice. The boy simply stared for a moment, then asked, "Have we been called or doomed?"

"Doom if we don't follow him," the man replied, grimacing at the bold blue stain. "If the chief bonereader of the Thrani wants to see us, we *go*."

"Now?"

"Now."

Taddin casually turned and set off across the plaza, knowing they would follow.

Bonereaders Court was an enclave within the wider enclave of the Thrani Quarter, a place apart. Tall houses shadowed a courtyard strewn with flower petals, some curling dry, some crushed underfoot, speckling the pavement like spilled coins. Each house had an arched doorway topped with a crude carved figure: luck-beasts, tamed demons, effigies of defeated enemies.

Taddin stopped before the highest, most imposing arch (its carved figure silently screaming, wings curving up behind the contorted form), and shrilled like a cicada. At once the door opened. A shrouded servant beckoned them in.

When Stilpin looked back, Taddin Whistle had gone.

They followed the servant down corridors whose gloom gradually became a twilit realm of hanging lamps, curtained doorways, and the stale reek of incense overlaying a darker smell of burning.

Stilpin had visited a bonereader once, just from curiosity when he had a few loose orrins in his pocket. The oracle had thrust a green bone, slender as a sapling, into the fire, for a reading so ambiguous it could have meant anything. He'd gone away half thrilled, half disappointed. But Santha Seona—you had to be rich as sin to see the Santha. Unless the Santha wanted to see you. . . . He entered the audience chamber with a dry mouth.

The wealth of it stunned the eye. On every wall, hangings winked with jewels. The lamps were elaborate confections of crystal and gold. The ceiling writhed with carvings, painted boldly in scarlet, silver, blue. No sign of soot from oracular fires, though the air had a faint after-scent of burning. At the far end of the room a platform rose on four squat, spiral posts, bearing a thronelike chair half-visible behind filigree screens. In the chair, something stirred as they approached.

"Sers, won't you sit before us?" A honey-sweet, lilting voice.

Low stools awaited them. Sitting, they must crouch in the attitude of supplicants. Stilpin's long legs angled awkwardly, while Tib seemed poised and unperturbed.

"You have been in our thoughts," the Santha said. "Trader in scraps from the mages' table." There was a knife's edge under the sweetness. "You and the foreign woman."

The breath tightened in Stilpin's throat. Seona didn't know the percept was here beside him. *Sers*, she had called them. How long until she found Tib out?

"To meddle with relics, broken toys—what harm in it? A very, very little, ser trader, the merest nothing." Seona graced the phrase with a ripple of laughter. Then the bone-reader's voice made an alarming swoop from treble to harsh baritone: "But to meddle with false prophets is an affront to the gods."

Shaken, Stilpin blurted the first thought that entered his head. "False? It came true, didn't it?"

"Chance." Now a neutral tenor, the Santha's tone was flat. "Only the bones sift truth from falsehood. Bones and the righteous fire."

"What do you want me to do?" No bravado from Stilpin now. Let him take the heat while Moabet sat unnoticed.

"Bring me the woman," Seona declared.

"Consider it done." Tib stood and approached the throne chair, while Stilpin bit back a cry of anguish. Tib—no, Moabet damnit, *Moabet*—faced the concealed bonereader with shoulders squared, then bent in a brisk, unwomanly bow. "Honorable Santha. I am at your service."

Through the screens, across the length of the glittering chamber, Stilpin could sense an intense scrutiny trained on the percept. A regard of equal fixity met the Santha. Stilpin almost expected to hear the clash of distant steel.

Then Moabet broke the silence. "Will you read the bones for me?"

Seona must have given a start of surprise. The chair creaked with the sudden movement of a massive form. But the reply was silken-smooth. "Which bones?"

"The oldest bones and the blackest fire," Moabet answered. Something odd about her voice, as if she spoke from a dream and stood awake, the two at once, enspelled yet wary.

Something rustled behind the screen. Then a heavy arm thrust through an opening. The arm was blue with sacred ideographs inked into the skin, while the palm glowed russet with henna. It curved, beckoned.

Moabet took a step forward, and came within reach of the bonereader's fingers. They rose like a flower on a thick stalk, bent to brush the percept's brow and lips, then jerked away as if seized by a gust of wind.

"*Sfeirr-asharh.*" The sound seemed to writhe in the air. It held awe, a hint of terror. Sensitive to every nuance in the Santha's voice, Stilpin was sure of this as he was of the power in the unknown word. The Santha was going to let them go.

Even as the thought came to him, the bonereader spoke with a brittle composure. "The interview is ended." They were dismissed.

The servant who had led them to the room reappeared to conduct them back. She (for this, at least, was unambiguously a woman beneath the veils) carried plain cloaks to cover their dye-spattered clothes.

As they left Bonereaders Court, a cry sounded in Santha Seona's chambers. "Mdessa, Kiri—ready the fires!"

"Which bones, Santha?"

"The old bones, fool! And bring the black *khur*—and a mantle. It will be a long night."

For all of us, Mdessa thought as she scurried to fetch the Santha's warmest cloak. Black *khur*! A shudder ran through her. Already the air seemed heavy with thunder and the scent of death.

V

The Maker

For one month out of the year, Xalycis Rock became a fortress under siege. In deep summer, the desert came to try the Rock's defenses with its arsenal of heat and drought, wind and sand. The outlying farms were already a wasteland of parched fields. No caravans came. The city lived on its reserves of food, its closely guarded reservoirs. Low City taverns raised the price of beer, while Wallwalk grandees idled away their evenings over wine. Outside, the wind hissed under a burden of sand. Days dawned blood red.

The Council ended its session in a welter of acrimony. One of its last acts was the granting of a license for an inn on Wallwalk, over the protest of neighbors to the former Nerra House. The Artifact had not been recovered. Berec i-Arnix's reward for news of his brother went unclaimed. The Vinculine of the Low City called up his private cadre of guards to assist the Helm in keeping the peace. Tempers had grown short in Xalycis.

Arriving at Vuorn House on a night without stars or wind,

when sullen heat abided in the stones, Stilpin pressed past the doorman with a mutter that could have been greeting or curse, and went in search of Moabet Shar. Unshaven, scowling, tunic damp with sweat, he was no sight to gladden the heart.

He found the percept in Vuorn's smaller perfume chamber, keeping its fans in motion with one hand while she held a book close under her nose, reading by a single flickering lamp.

"You'll go blind," he said.

She closed the book but kept the fans moving. "You've been to Lowtown again." Head cocked slightly, eyes heavy-lidded, she went on: "In a tavern—asking questions." Then her eyes opened wide and her fingers tightened on the cord. "You've found him, haven't you? The renegade chemic."

Stilpin's jaw clenched. He was a most reluctant bearer of news. After the incident at Bonereaders Court, he didn't owe her anything, of course. All bets were off. So it must have been the challenge of tracking the mock-relicts to their source that had driven him on, then brought him here. Now his thoughts were a chaos of half-formed plans and swiftly rehearsed lies, all dissolving under her gaze. Gods help him, he was going to tell her the truth again.

"Yes." The word stuck in his throat.

There it came, that expectant silence. The faint creaking of the fans rubbed against his nerves. Even the artificial breeze was an unwelcome intimacy.

"Damn you for making me do this, he's Sandhound's maker," he said in a rush.

It was done. Now the relentless memory would come into play. If she'd ever heard of Sandhound, the most fleeting, offhand reference, the percept would retrieve it. He watched her with a sour appreciation.

"Owner of The Broken Man. An inn—Tumbleside?"

Well, at least she didn't know everything. "It's over the line, right in the Tumbles."

"Why would anyone go there?"

Better and better. He could almost pretend he was enjoying himself, enlightening an ignorant outlander.

Then she spoiled it by answering her own question. "The thrill of danger. Relict diggers not far away—another lure. And something else. . . ."

No, he wouldn't speak this time. Let her work the rest of it out.

"*Calasta*," she said. "*Khur*. Snakeweed. Dreamsmoke and *alal*. Active essences."

Stilpin gave her an ironic salute.

She leaned forward, letting the fans fall still. "When do we go?"

"We don't."

"You think it's too dangerous?"

"That's right." He looked her square in the face, expecting to see a furious resolve forming. Instead he encountered— what was it? She turned before he had a chance to decide.

Moabet drew out a sheaf of scent wands. There was a rack at one side of the chamber with flasks of essences neatly arrayed. She selected several, opened them, and charged the wands with practiced efficiency, then sent him another enigmatic glance. "Turn your back."

"What?" Lost in confusion, he did as he was bid.

Cloth rustled. His mind filled with a vision of Moabet slipping out of her clothes. If she couldn't argue him from his resolve, did she intend to seduce him? Thinking he was easy game, hungry for her charms? Then she was in for a rude awakening.

"All right. It's done."

He swung around, heart pounding.

Tib stood where the percept had been. There was something

odd about the brat. More than usually exasperating. Was it the sly glint in the eye, a new shiftiness, a sense that this clerkling could not possibly be trusted? Why had he ever hired such an unpleasant boy anyway?

The whirl of questions froze. Stilpin struggled to regain the power of speech. Finally he managed to whisper, "How did you do that?"

"A notion I'm trying out: use a perfume portrait as a mask. Placing the essence directly on the skin seems to heighten the effect."

Unnerving to hear Moabet's voice issuing from this creature. Stilpin clasped his hands behind him to hide their trembling, and tried to gather his wits. For a moment he could not even remember what they had been talking about before Tib appeared.

"I have one for you too. A perfume mask." Tib was busy with wands and flasks again. "Can you do a Wallwalk accent? It would help."

This was a dream, that was the only explanation. Reality had lost its moorings. Stilpin surrendered to the madness. "Accent? Dear child, what other way *is* there to speak?" he inquired with a grandee's languid grace.

"Good. Now take off your tunic."

Bemused, he obeyed. The scent wands flicked over him like darting insects, a sting of cool essence at his throat, breastbone, armpits, waist. At least he did not have to suffer the boy's grubby fingers on his skin.

"Boring, isn't it?" Tib asked with a slight catch in his voice. "You find such attentions tedious, even from your page."

Stilpin sensed what was expected of him. "Oh, quite. But one can hardly attend to such matters oneself," he drawled.

"Perfect! That's just the tone." Tib tossed the discarded tunic back to him. "It will work. You'll see."

At the moment, Stilpin saw nothing at all, but he'd had enough of questions. Maybe this dream would release him soon, and he could sink back into simple sleep.

The lampman stopped where the lane vanished under an ancient pile of rubble. A narrow track ran off to the right, lit by torches on tall poles bearing a strange emblem, halfway between a bent crosspiece and a distorted human form. Beyond, the patchwork plaster and lath facade of a large building rose against the night.

"Far as I go." He gestured toward the track. "Plenty of light." He held out his palm, waiting for payment.

"How the hell do I get back, then?" asked the Hightown swell petulantly, speech just a little slurred. He set a hand on his page's shoulder, steadying himself. "Most visitors don't leave till day?" he asked.

"Some stays, some doesn't. You're not stuck if you ain't suited." A grin, revealing rotted teeth, as the grandee doled out the fare and a bit over. "Thank you kindly, sir." And, with remarkable swiftness, he was gone.

"Sir?" The page took a step onto the path. A small, lithe youth dressed all in black, with a black pearl in his ear, he resembled a small, dark cat, scarcely visible in shadow.

Roused from a moment's brooding, the grandee strolled past him and led the way from Tumbleside into the ruins themselves and the outpost called The Broken Man.

The emblem on the torch poles was repeated on a sign hanging above the massive doors, but here there was no doubt of its meaning. The wrecked figure was realistic and grotesque—most of all its smile. Two unsmiling toughs flanked the doors.

"Your business?" one asked.

Casually, as if the phrase had just come to him: "A word with the Hound," the grandee said.

The toughs seemed not to have heard, for they gave no flicker of reaction. Then the page advanced bearing a square of black velvet on which lay four golden orrins. That brought a grin from the one with the bent, broken nose. He looked at the swell with a more friendly eye. "Hound'll like your style, gent. You have a name?"

"Ah . . . no. I don't believe I do."

"*He*'ll give you one, picked special." The other man held the door open. "Has a way with 'em, Sandhound does."

The grandee paused on the threshold. "Has he names for you?" The novelty of bantering with servants seemed to rouse him a little from his languor.

"Pursehole and Bender," came the answer in a woman's cool voice. "Come along, then, if you're ready."

Grandee and page followed a retreating billow of brocade into a torchlit expanse of peeling plaster and soiled, once-splendid rugs where footsteps made no sound. The sparse wall hangings and occasional bits of furniture in these halls had a scavenged look like the woman's gown, shot with fraying gold. She walked quickly, pale hair swinging in a heavy plait, making no effort to catch her visitor's fancy with courtesan's tricks. At the foot of a stairway, she finally paused and turned. "You're early, you know. He may be sleeping." Long nose and jaw, hooded eyes, a maiden's lips rosy and incongruous, adding up to an odd beauty. "I can offer you wine, but it goes bad quick out here. Too much corpse dust in the winds, sticks in your throat." Suddenly she laughed, a dry sound like crackling paper, fingers over her mouth.

"No wine, then. Might we risk disturbing Sandhound?"

Her shrug revealed a split along the shoulder of the gown. "Risk whatever you like. That's why you're here, isn't it?" She began to climb the stairs.

Though they saw no other people, there was an increasing

sense of presence: creaking wood—or a soft cry?—a murmuring of wind or voices, obscure thumpings.

"Vermin busy in the walls tonight," the woman declared with careless contempt.

The grandee asked no further explanation.

Coming to a door distinguished only by a scrawled glyph like a slash of paint, she rapped lightly with her knuckles. "Hound?"

The door ghosted open on oiled hinges, bringing a chill breath of old smoke from the room beyond. Sandhound sat in a high-backed chair, facing them, in an attitude of ease. It was at once apparent he was the woman's brother. A sallow man, hair and flesh much of a color, eyes like old ivory, the long nose and jaw exaggerated farther in him. He wore a suit of soft, pale leather, brindle with old stains.

"Laelis, love, who have you brought me?"

"Nameless and his footnote." She moved to stand beside him. They gazed at the visitors with an oddly inhuman stare, like two rare beasts.

"Nameless? That won't do." Sandhound considered a moment. "Shanks the Wall-Strider!"

The grandee, just settling into a chair, started and looked around him as though he would not have been surprised to see the legendary king of spiders clinging to the wall behind him.

Laelis covered her mouth again, amused.

"And the footnote," Sandhound continued, "he shall be . . . Flea." Giving no time for the page to protest, he cleared his throat. "So, Shanks. What can I do for you?"

"I need—" a gesture canceled the words. "I would like to sample certain pleasures beyond the comprehension of the law. To breathe . . ." an arch pause, "more interesting airs."

"Airs. Ah." A regal inclination of the head, followed by

a fanged grin. Sandhound became blunt. "Just what do you want?"

The grandee twisted a ring on his finger, watching how the stone caught the light. Then he looked up. "A little of everything you've got. So I'll know I've run the gamut."

"Bravo, Shanks, that's the boy! Try anything once— maybe you'll like it." Sandhound leaned forward slightly. "It'll cost you."

With the frown of a man unaccustomed to doing his own bargaining, "I daresay."

They came to terms after a tangle of Hightown hauteur and Lowtown arrogance sorted itself into the blander relation of client and purveyor. Goods and payment would change hands, at a date of mutual convenience. Sandhound was on the point of dismissing his visitors when the grandee said, with the sly shyness of a born fool, "I've heard you've a gifted maker."

"So? You want something else?"

"I—no, you would never agree."

"To what, Shanks?" Sandhound inquired, all patience.

The grandee's voice dropped to a husky whisper. "A look behind the scenes."

His page cried, "Master, no!" even as Laelis shook her head, "Impossible. Loft's off-limits."

"Well now, sister," Sandhound replied gently, "all things have their price. Say . . . fifty orrins?"

"*Hound!*"

The grandee considered it. Glanced at his page, registering the boy's evident fear. Lips quirked in a slight, unpleasant smile that transformed mere foolishness to practiced vice. "Done." The boy shivered under his hand.

Up two flights of increasingly rickety stairs, they came to a region where steps clattered on uncarpeted, creaking boards, and the air had a subtle stink of chemicrye. Sandhound ushered them through a low doorway into a vast, windy space of swaying light and crouched shadows. An extravagant chandelier hung from the center of the high ceiling, prisms restlessly chiming. It illuminated a chaos of baskets, jars, scrap metal, tools, strewn books, and shapeless bundles.

The grandee almost said it looked like a ransacked warehouse, but managed instead to declare, "Looks like your maker's not at home."

"He's around someplace. Hey, Chityr! Get your ass out here. You've got visitors."

A tall, gaunt form rose from a tangle of equipment like a summoned spirit. "Why, thank you, Sandhound. It's been so long since I've seen a new face." A dreamy voice, shading into vague mutterings as Chityr bent again, "I know I put it somewhere. Cloudy Dust. No, not that one. Here, is this it?" He peered into an open cask. "I'd forgotten about these." Chityr straightened, holding out a palm filled with fine beads of opalescent glass small as insect eggs. Suddenly he flung them into the air. Sandhound flinched, but the glittering shower fell harmlessly.

Chityr smiled. "I'd like to see the clouds open and pour them all over the city like broken rainbows. I saw it in a dream."

Laelis muttered something disrespectful under her breath as Sandhound crunched through the beads toward Chityr.

"New friends for you, hey? Shanks and Flea—house names, of course." Sandhound winked. "Take a good look, so you'll give Shanks your best. He wants the works. Check the body type, figure the dilutions, all that chemic's cant you're always going on about. Bring out his *soul*, Chityr."

The grandee could not suppress an apprehensive shifting of the eyes under the maker's gaze. The page, scrutinized as well, remained nonchalant. Whatever the chemic saw in them (souls or otherwise), his expression remained benevolent.

After a moment he remembered his manners as well, and gave a rusty bow. "Honored, ser. Lodvin Chityr, at your service." He glanced again at the page, with a slight frown, but said nothing further.

"There will be no difficulties, I trust?" the grandee finally asked.

"No, none at all. That is, the essences may balk a bit, they do that—not wanting to make the effort and come alive, you know. But I'll take them in hand. Treat them right, they'll do whatever you want."

Sandhound reasserted himself. "You need anything, let me know." Then, as though the maker had ceased to exist, he turned back to the grandee and amiably but firmly led him from the loft, trailed by Laelis and the page.

"He didn't trust us."

"We were strangers. And the scent masks were too crude. I've worked on them, borrowing more from Vuorn's portraits, and next time they'll stand up to anyone's scrutiny. Sandhound will believe his senses then, before he accepts his chemic's judgment. Odd type to find in the Tumbles, that Chityr, didn't you think?"

"Don't change the subject."

The argument continued at varying levels of intensity for the next few days. It had reached no resolution the evening before their scheduled return to complete the transaction.

"Moabet. I know Vuorn's not the sort to break the rules, and Dalu thinks only a drum-priest should handle actives. I'm willing to help you get around them. You can play with"— hastily Stilpin corrected himself, under her basilisk glare— "*experiment* with scent masks till you're satisfied they work, and I'll try them out for you—I'll walk naked through the markets at high noon if you want. Then I can go rob a warehouse somewhere, get you just what you asked for."

"But you won't go back to The Broken Man."

"Damn it, yes. I will. All right? *Alone*."

"If you go, I'll follow you. My presence raises the odds in our favor, don't you see? If Sandhound doesn't play this straight, I can guess his options."

"While I blunder in the dark." Stilpin's tone was icy. "And then you make the first mistake of your life—or I fall to pieces, whatever you like—and they bash our heads in. Easy to get rid of a corpse or two in the Tumbles. Just find a digger's pit or a suitable heap of rubble. All done, no questions asked."

"To get anywhere, we have to face risks."

"Men do. It's different for women. You're so—" he paused a moment at the rage in her eyes, but went on regardless, "so vulnerable. Can you get the better of Sandhound in a fight? Never mind his men. Tib might grow strong and tall enough to hold his own someday—you won't. And I've heard about those fighting women in the eastern lands, so don't start in about them. They're a thousand miles from Xalycis; you're stuck here with the sand winds blowing and a lot of angry drunkards in the streets, crazies in the Tumbles. You plan to get through all that, fox your way into The Broken Man, and buy enough actives to send all the thieves in the city straight to heaven. Well I say *no*! It's not going to happen. I'll get Dalu to lock you in the storerooms if I have to. Understand?"

He had been yelling. She simply looked at him, the flush of anger already gone from her cheeks. Stilpin knew then that the battle was lost, though he would keep on fighting it to the bitter end.

Sandhound met them at the door of The Broken Man, wearing a cloak thrown over his brindle leather. "Shanks! You've got the damnedest luck. No—don't come in. Listen."

He moved out onto the front walk and they trailed after him. "Chityr's made the actives, great work. He's an artist. But —and I wasn't going to tell you this—there's a thing he can't do. Black *khur*, like the bonereaders use. Twice the power of red *khur*. Secret process, special ingredients."

He wielded the words like a charm, leading grandee and page away from the building into the huge tract of rubble, dim shapes lit by the torch in his hand and by distant flecks of fire where relict diggers guarded their claims. "Here's where the luck comes in. I found a source. Can you believe it? Man walks into the place, says he's got something to show me." Sandhound paused for effect, then threw back his head and gave a wild, yipping howl, chilling in the desolation of the Tumbles. "I tell you, Shanks, it was *the best*. Just about blew my head off."

At last Stilpin broke the flow of speech. "If he offered it then, why don't you have it on hand now? It would save us this tramping about." He gave a refined shudder and looked longingly back toward The Broken Man, now hidden behind a great slumping mound.

"Dragon god wouldn't like it. Has to be a ceremony." Sandhound chuckled. "Craziest religion you've ever seen, and that's saying a lot for this city. Harmless, though. Bunch of loonies as far into dreamland as Chityr."

"Why did they let you try their *khur* without . . . initiation, whatever it is?"

A soft laugh. "You're a thinking man, Shanks. I like that. Thing is, I *am* initiate. Not a god in Xalycis doesn't know my name—and give me a listen too." Oddly, he seemed to mean it. Sandhound was genuinely proud of his special relationship with higher powers. He stopped for a moment, swiveling to face the grandee. "You worried for your orrins, Shanks? Hell, all you're carrying's a nice, safe bank note. I know it and you know it. So nobody's going to rob you.

Think of it as an *honor*. You'll be the only initiate on the Walk. A Dragon Man! How's that sound?''

Moabet's chill fingers danced for a moment in Stilpin's palm. Hand cant. *We can handle it*. She moved away before he could reply in kind.

So he summoned his courage, and made one last attempt to gauge Sandhound's plans. ''What are they doing out here, these Dragon Men of yours? Hell of a place to stage ceremonies.''

''Ah, but it makes perfect sense.'' Sandhound's voice sank. ''You see, they think they're mages, on their way back to glory. So they stick to the old haunts.''

Stilpin moved on automatically, wooden with shock. Someone had found the Artifact out here—how did they know it was a survival, not a new-made thing? If Moabet had the mage-power in her, she might meet her own kind tonight. Sweat broke cold on his brow, though he knew his imagination was taking wild leaps.

Again, Moabet's hand touched his. No message this time but simple reassurance. She quickly broke the contact and fell back to walk behind him, quiet in soft boots.

The Tumbles seemed enormous, too large for the confines of Xalycis Rock. Legend said this had been a second crest, fanged with jutting crags, uninhabitable, until the mages blasted it to a plateau and built their wondrous private city. By torchlight and the glimmer of the stars, the fallen walls appeared by turns magically whole and transformed back into raw cliffs. How did Sandhound find his way, where even Time seemed lost and wandering?

''This'll be it. Watch your head.''

The mound displayed a dark opening like a burrow. If any light came from within, it was lost in the torch's glare. A low tunnel led downward at a steep angle. Vacant. If the would-be mages had set guards, Stilpin could detect no signs of them as he descended at an awkward crouch.

Then the stench rose up to meet him. The tunnel bent and widened into a chamber of blue fires, strewn garbage, and figures out of nightmare. They towered, hair piled in wild rats' nests and twisted into spiraling horns. The blue light winked on jewels half hidden in bramble beards, jewels adorning rags and dirt-blackened flesh. One naked man had wrapped his dangling genitals in ropes of gold and pearls.

Sandhound greeted them with enviable calm. "The supplicant. Ah, and a servant with him. Hope you don't object."

One of the grotesques stepped forward. "We welcome all believers. May all men enter the Dragon's fire and be changed." The formal words were spoken in the cracked, coarse voice of madness.

"The Dragon's fire," the others droned in chorus.

"Come, Shanks, let go your boy. He won't be harmed." Sandhound waved them forward. "Remember the rewards of faith." He grinned, clearly enjoying himself.

"You must be pure in the sight of the Dragon," the leader intoned. Without warning, he cast a packet of white powder onto one of the fires, and thick smoke billowed.

"Breathe deep." A claw-fingered hand grasped Stilpin by the hair and thrust his face into the choking fumes. Eyes streaming, he could not tell if Moabet had been seized as well. He reached out blindly, to recoil at the touch of dry flesh. Then, he was floating like a paper lantern caught in a rising wind, terrified and laughing. Sounds swirled around him: rhythmic chanting in an unknown tongue, and above it a high howling. Sandhound?

The howls became terrified barks. Stilpin opened his eyes to a black wave of vertigo. When his vision cleared, he wished that it had not. Three men crouched over the still-twitching body of a gaunt Tumbleside dog with its throat slit, blood pumping out in a dark spray. He thought he would vomit, but instead he began to float again, suspended in a warm, glittering firmament that embraced him and teased away the horror from his heart. Where was Moabet? She should join him. They could dance together on air, and afterward—a vivid image of lust and possession leapt in him. He fumbled at his clothes, but his hands were dissolving, he was vanishing now in the shining, the sweet odor of blood.

A startled oath broke into his trance. He knew it for Sand-hound's voice. But hadn't he been changed into a dog and slaughtered? Stilpin's muzzy speculations halted abruptly as he saw what had drawn the oath.

It was the image of a man limned in golden light, in glory. Before him, the believers—pitiful, ragged creatures now, void of all threat—sank down in worship.

The Glowing Man was beckoning. Unsteadily, Stilpin approached. Someone was advancing beside him, a boy with blood in his hair and eyes that caught the golden light as though they burned from within. The shining fingers drifted toward them. Then Stilpin's wrist was seized in a solid human grasp, and he was pulled forward as a whisper sounded in his ear: "Don't say a word. Just come with me." Bewildered, he obeyed.

No others but himself and the boy followed the apparition into the chill slap of night air, the sudden darkness where the Glowing Man burned brighter.

"Quick as you can," it said. "No time to waste." Then it set out at a long-legged stride, and they stumbled after.

When it finally slowed its pace, Stilpin had a stitch in his side and a pain in one ankle, but he had returned to something like his right mind—even if it countenanced the existence of solid, golden ghosts.

The apparition was trying to catch its breath, ribs heaving under shining skin. Could visions have gooseflesh?

"Oh," a gulp for air. "That was splendid!" The glow was fading now, to dull red embers.

"Yes it was." Moabet stood, smiling back. "Thank you, Chityr, for rescuing us."

Lodvin Chityr, sublimely unconscious of his nudity, made a neat bow. "Best thing I could think of, when Hound said what he had in mind. I didn't like the sound of it."

"Here, you'd better have this. And my thanks as well." Stilpin offered his cloak, which came to Chityr's bony knees. "Is it safe for you to go back to The Broken Man?"

"Oh, I'm not," airily. "Got my goods out yesterday, the important ones. And your samples. I'll go into hiding till this blows over. Rather not face Hound for a while."

Could this blithe creature evade determined pursuit? Well, he'd made it this far.

Stilpin shivered, momentarily regretting the loan of his cloak. "What I'd give for a hot bath! Get the stink of that place out of my clothes." He suddenly remembered the blood in Moabet's hair, and turned to her in alarm. "Dear gods, were you hurt?"

"No. Truly, I'm all right. That bath sounds good, though."

Chityr had an inspiration. "There's a sandbath down in Saltmary Lane, open all night. Nothing better than sand to take the chill from your bones. I suppose I should get this pigment off before it stiffens." He reached under the cloak and meditatively scratched his chest.

Stilpin realized it must be some version of the substance that gave the mock-relicts their shifting hues. Then it came to him that Sandhound's runaway maker was worth fortunes, a walking treasure house. He groaned, "Gods help us," and pulled off his silken neck cloth. "Here, use this on the worst of it. Do they know you at this sandbath? Moabet, give him your cap.''

The burly doorkeeper rented them a private bath with absolute indifference. In the dim, warm chamber, Chityr immediately flung off cloak and cap and immersed himself in the shallow pit of sand, humming with satisfaction. Stilpin undressed with a more furtive haste, eyes carefully averted from Moabet, but when he sank into the sand he heaved a sigh, smiled, and looked up to see a rounded hip, the shadowed movement of a breast close beside him. A drop of sweat trickled down along her ribs, slowly, as though it deliberately lingered.

Around the edge of the bath was a padded ledge where bathers could retreat when the sand's heat grew too intense. Niches held stone jars of oil, and shell scrapers. After a few minutes, the chemic pulled himself up.

"This has been an interesting day," he remarked. Then, turning to Stilpin, "I owe you thanks, sir. I'd grown used to Hound, and you reminded me that I truly don't like the man. Oh, you may call it a hasty judgment. There's good to him, bound to be." His glance drifted to Moabet. "Here, child. Don't stay in too long at first."

When Chityr beckoned her out of the sand, Stilpin didn't know whether to curse or bless him. Heart racing, he followed.

The chemic began to speak of baths in all their variety, eyes dreamy, one foot trailing in the sand. "Milk. Now that seems such a waste, to bathe in it. Better to create the *illusion* of milk." He swung his arm in a gesture indicating the simplicity of such chemicrye. "Odd, how we think of milk as a cool summer luxury, when we all first sucked it warm from the teat." He gave Moabet a nod of benign acknowledgment. Stilpin made a soft, choking sound and shifted his position on the ledge.

Chityr returned to his original theme. "Water has a pleasing buoyancy, but I like the weight of sand, the way it touches everything as though it's curious about you."

Moabet scooped a handful of sand, regarded it for a moment, then let it drift down onto Stilpin's leg. A muscle jumped in his thigh.

"Torment, of course, if you're ticklish," the chemic added. He looked around in surprise as his companions burst into crazy laughter.

It still sputtered from them when they were gulping for air, eyes streaming, arms on each other's shoulders. It shook their throats, trapped, as their mouths met in a long, hilarious, desperate kiss.

Chityr eased back into the sand. He basked in the warmth, drowsy now, though his mind still roamed and pondered. Whose chemicrye had disguised these charming lovers so well until they entered the bath, stripping off their old identities with their clothes? And what did they want with active essences? Black *khur*, now. . . . He glanced toward the scatter of garments where the woman's jacket lay. She hadn't seen the dog-killer slipping the flask into her pocket as the Golden Man led them away from the debauchery that would have followed their initiation. Active essences were one thing, a blood feast quite another. Chityr, the maker who had cheerfully sampled most of his wares, recoiled from blood and its odor of cruelty—the darkest essence of all. There was no cruelty about this pair, he was sure of it. Look, now, how they drew apart as though they'd frightened themselves with their ardor. Charming!

VI

Dancer's Fortune

Berec i-Arnix had never known such discomfort. Swaddled in wind scarves and cloak, eyes slitted against the stinging gusts, he made his way along a narrow street that seemed composed entirely of obstacles: slouched beggars underfoot, porters heedless of whom they might barge into with their misshapen bales and sharp-edged boxes, running children (out at this hour in such weather!), and the constant presence of the wind.

He rubbed a bruised shoulder and cursed the impulse that had led him to come himself on this fool's errand. Too late to turn back though. Here he was on the doorstep of the inn, its heavy sign jerking overhead with each gust. The Dancing Dog indeed! With a snort of disgust, the head of clan Arnix rapped on the door.

An old man peered out. "Don't stand there gaping, fellow. Want to bring the whole storm in with you?"

Once inside, Berec unwrapped his wind scarves in dignified

silence, releasing a shower of fine sand onto a floor already thick with grit. Every footstep crunched.

"Guildmaster of the Artists Vagabond at your service," the old man proclaimed.

Such charlatan grandeur from a doorman! Berec responded with a coldly correct nod and introduced himself with the single word "Arnix."

"What about him? Any word?" the guildmaster asked.

"*I* am Arnix," Berec corrected. Was the old man senile?

"Ah. The brother. Out searching for him yourself now, are you? It's a sad thing when families split asunder."

Berec ignored the insolent familiarity. At least the fellow hadn't lost all his wits. He stopped at the head of a short stairway. "I'm told there's a performer called Knifedancer who can be contacted here. This gentleman did not see fit to inform me that he was the last known person to see my brother, but that omission has finally been rectified. I wish to speak to him. Is he here?"

It happened that Railu was. Since the call for performers had gone out from the new Wallwalk inn (still making ready for its gala opening), Artists Vagabond had begun to drift into the Dancing Dog with unusual frequency, casting each other dark looks and trying to discover what new acts were in the works. Sandwind season, to make matters worse. The Dog had witnessed two fistfights already, and one frightening game of bluff with the broken shards of tankards. The guildmaster thanked his gods that Knifedancer had an easy temper. Still, he was on the point of denying that Railu ever came near the place—this pompous grandee likely didn't mean him any good—when a cry went up from the common room: "Hey, Dancer! Stand us a round or we'll boot you into next week."

Berec's bland brown eyes sharpened. "I take it that's the man I'm after?"

The hell with it. The guildmaster indicated the stairs. "Go on down, join the fun. You've found him."

It took Berec some time to adjust to the dimness. His informant had described the Shandar clearly enough, but no one could pick him out of this disorderly rabble. Revolted by the odor of stale spilt beer, Berec raised the edge of his cloak a fastidious inch above the floor and moved closer.

"C'mon, Railu," someone said in slurred, wheedling tones. "You've got something up your sleeve beside a few cutters. Or d'you think the Blue Lion's hot for that old routine with the knives: up, down, over, under—'Hey, he's gonna slice off his prick,' 'Nope, he didn't.' And under, around, and up and back. That'll play big up on the Walk."

Guffaws greeted these witticisms. The one not laughing, yes, that must be the Shandar. Berec wondered if he would have time to question the fellow. A brawl could explode at any moment.

Then Knifedancer shrugged. "Guess I'll just have to drop my britches and give the Quality a good look." He rested his hands on his lean hips and grinned at his tormentor. "So fuck off, Kolb. Go work on your own show-stopper."

Kolb shot back an obscenity in return, but without rancor. The knot of Artists Vagabond began to disperse. Berec followed Knifedancer to a table by the far wall.

"I'd like to speak with you. If you'll permit . . . ?"

"Pull up a chair." Railu sprawled with one boot on the table. "Do I know you or something?"

"You knew—*know*—my brother. Gherifan Arnix." Berec watched intently for signs of guilt, but the Shandar merely sighed.

"That goddam bastard. I miss him. Don't know why, the way he ran out on us."

" 'Us'?"

"This bunch." Railu made a comprehensive gesture. "His

friends.'' Then he looked Berec up and down with some scorn. ''Only ones he had, from what I hear.''

The interview was not going at all as Berec had planned. He tried to regain the upper hand. ''Commendable loyalty, my good man, but the word is you could find him now if you wished.''

Knifedancer's green eyes turned a shade colder. ''Whose word is that?''

Hastily, Berec went on. ''Don't forget, there's profit to be made from what you know. His family wants him back.'' Now that might bring him around. The Shandar was just too lazy to go after the reward without a kick in the pants. Berec sat back and waited.

He was too astonished to put up a struggle when Railu Knifedancer hoisted him from his chair, propelled him into the hallway, and said with tired disgust, ''Get this piece of garbage out of here.'' Before he knew it, Berec was in the street, buffeted by a derisive wind. Fiasco! Arranged by one of his family's enemies no doubt, just to humiliate him. Well, let that put an end to it. Gherifan Arnix was dead and buried. Withdraw the reward, pass a few delicate hints that sad news had come his way, and to perdition with his brother.

Berec suffered a moment's qualms. What if Gherifan were in some trouble, thinking himself beyond help? But no, he must harden his heart. Let Gherifan make his way out of his own messes. Perhaps the young idiot was happy just as he was, homeless, penniless, cut adrift. Berec thrust out his jaw. So be it. He would wash his hands of the whole affair.

That night Railu lay alone on a borrowed bed upstairs at the Dog, thinking about Gherifan Arnix. It had been easy to let things slide and just assume Gherro had cut out on the first caravan. But that was already late in the season. The pickings would be slim. Had he been so desperate to leave?

You couldn't blame him, with a brother like that. Still, Railu had a feeling, call it a hunch or a piece of dream-knowledge, but he could not get it out of his mind. Gherro was here in Xalycis.

Railu recalled that last night at the wake. They had been talking about old Arnix's killer. Some nonsense Railu himself had brought up—the duty of revenge. Hellfire, what a thing to say to a man with his father just murdered! Railu cursed himself for a fool. Had he set Gherro off on some mad quest? If he'd had any sense, he would have told him to go talk to that girl who made the prophecy.

Impossible to sleep. It was hot as all damnation tonight, sand in the sheets. Railu lit a candle and began to dress. Just get the hell out, go for a walk. Or home to the Valley, look up Grand-uncle and ask him what had happened to the girl. What was her name? Moabet. With the name came a memory. Vuorn House: they'd know there. And Dalu might be staying over. Funny, how he'd never thought to look up Grand-uncle's employer on the Walk. Had those midnight tours of Arnix House been too much for a Shandar lad?

A plan of action formed. Discover where Moabet had gone, then go and coax her into doing her famous party trick again. *Look into my eyes, girl, and tell me where Gherro went. Maybe a dream already told me and I just can't bring it clear.*

He flung a cloak over his shoulder, stuffed a wind scarf in his pocket, and strode out into the uneasy peace of the night. Gherro had taught him the back ways up to Wallwalk, so there was no problem with the guardpost. By the time he could hear the Arnix banner bells mingling with the jangling of Vuorn's the next house over, Railu was in high humor. An image of the percept in her Shandar gear lightened his way, and he felt the luck running with him. He knocked at Vuorn's door as though he had every right to be there with dawn just beginning to pale the eastern sky.

A yawning servant opened the door a crack. "What do you want?"

"Is the chemic here?"

The man's eyes widened and he tried to close the door, but Railu's boot was firmly lodged. "Dalu Chemic," Railu said with elaborate patience. "I'm his grand-nephew. Heard he was here," he added at a venture.

The fear went out of the servant all at once. (So what had set him off then?) With an informality born of relief, the early hour, and an obvious familiarity with Knifedancer's name, the man let him in, gesturing for quiet. Railu expected to be led to the back kitchen to wait for Dalu, but he was ushered to a formal dining room instead. Candlelight gleamed on an elegant table already set with silver. Weren't they afraid he'd grab the lot and bolt? There was something strange going on at Vuorn House.

Soft-footed, Railu made his way along the corridors until he found the kitchen. Forbidden ground? If so, he would damned well find out why.

The room smelled like paradise—fresh bread, and something sizzling on a spit over the main hearth. Off in one corner, a gangling fellow was munching on a bread roll with a look of foolish contentment.

"Good day to you," Railu hailed him. "Or nearly day. Any more of that around?"

The fellow passed him a basket of rolls still warm from the oven, and declared, "I'd forgotten the benefits of living in a well-kept home. Of course, everything depends on the people there. And do you know, that's another thing I seem to have forgotten? The importance of good companions."

Who was this zany anyway? He didn't sound like a servant. Railu introduced himself.

"Ah, Knifedancer. Dalu's told me about you. Lodvin Chityr."

The name meant nothing to Railu. He'd been too preoccupied of late to catch any rumors that Sandhound's maker had gone missing.

"I rescued my rescuers and they brought me here," Lodvin explained. "Stilpin gave me his own cloak to wear, which was good of him since I hadn't any clothes on at the time."

Railu laughed. "Well, it looks like you're in clover now, Chityr. Linen on your back and good bread in your hand. What more could a man want?"

The rhetorical question went unanswered. The sound of a familiar, solid tread brought Railu away from the hearth to meet his grand-uncle as he was entering the room.

Dalu cuffed him lightly. "So there you are, whelp. I should have known you'd get into mischief the moment you arrived."

"Mischief?" Railu glanced back at Chityr, then faced Dalu again. "Just what are *you* up to?"

Following his nose, Dalu found the rolls. Chityr was removing a chicken from the spit, his movements surprisingly deft. Railu gave him another look. Chityr met it with a sunny smile. "Have some?"

When Vuorn came down to breakfast, he found his new guest, the renegade chemic, chatting merrily with the two Shandar, as the cook tried to shoo them out of her kitchen.

They were six at table that morning, three of them on their second breakfasts. Sworn to secrecy regarding Chityr's whereabouts, Railu joined in the talk like a familiar friend of the house. Chityr seemed thoroughly accepted as well. And the percept! (Finding her here was a sure sign that the gods were with him today.) Something had changed in her since the time in Ladder Valley—not just the cropped hair. From her smile, and Stilpin's glower at Railu when he dared address her, the answer became obvious. The lady had a lover. Part of Railu's mind considered mischief (Ser Stilpin was so anxiously besotted!), but he determined to stick to business. At the first fitting moment, he brought up the matter of Gherro's disappearance.

"Young Gherifan? I was the one first sent him to the players," Dalu said. "Better your drunken owl-catchers and fire eaters than Aubric i-Arnix, eh?" A chuckle. "The way that boy would sit on the boundary wall and mimic me! Not an ounce of respect."

There was a moment's dumbstruck silence as Railu tried to imagine that scene. Then he found the thread of his subject again, and told of his meeting with Berec i-Arnix.

"So you're trying to track the boy down?"

Railu gave a curt nod. "He could be in trouble."

His listeners forbore to say that if Gherifan Arnix had run into trouble, it might be far too late for rescue.

Stilpin asked Vuorn for the butter, and the master of Vuorn House passed it down without the intervention of a servant. With an absent nod of thanks, Stilpin said, "He's probably snug in some beauty's bed, and scant gratitude he'd give you for dragging him out of it."

Railu shrugged. He was still wondering at the casual manners at this table, the easy association between high-born and low. Vuorn was formal enough, impressive even, with his old-fashioned beard and solemn eyes. Still, you could tell he and his chemic were old friends, not master and man. Chityr? Something between a favored son and the house jester, indulged, admired, and laughed at by turns. He seemed to be Dalu's 'prentice, as Moabet was Vuorn's. Surely some of these remarkable folk could help him now. "Gherifan liked the ladies right enough, but he wasn't in those sorts of spirits when I last saw him."

The percept had become interested in Knifedancer's rambling tale. "What kind of man is Gherifan?" She turned to Vuorn. "He was a neighbor—did you ever do a portrait?"

"Not of any Arnix. The patriarch thought it was nonsense, and refused to let his family come to me for such a purpose."

" 'Mumbo jumbo and rosewater,' he called it." Dalu made a sound of disgust. "Man should have been out on the plains in a breechclout, riding trash horses and collecting heads. At least the younger son was different."

"Different every time you meet him," Railu put in. "Tragedy, smiles, hermit, lady killer. That time he ran away with our troupe, he worked up this Low Town character, Leandric Gath. Got so none of us trusted him with the takings, till he fell for one of the singing girls and changed his ways again."

"How old was he then?" Moabet asked.

"Eighteen? No, seventeen it was. Six years ago." Railu stared into his cup of moka. "Best summer of his life, he claimed afterward."

They had forgotten Lodvin Chityr, and were startled when he spoke. "That boy should meet my mother. She's just the same. Except she ran to the players and didn't come back."

"What's her name?" Railu asked. "I never heard of a Chityr in the Artists."

"Oh, no, that was Father. She just used the one name, Margola."

All around the table, jaws dropped.

Dalu was the first to speak. "Not the Goddess herself? The Red Lily?"

"Well," Lodvin seemed embarrassed. "Yes. They used to call her things like that."

Vuorn's expression had grown vague as he looked into his own memories. "Her portrait stays forever young." He left the rest of the thought unspoken, but Lodvin obviously caught the feeling behind the words.

"Mother is still—striking, you know. I found it a bit difficult when I was younger. Father just laughed." Lodvin gave an awkward dip of the head. "He's dead now. She was sad, but . . ." The words trailed off, and for a moment no one spoke.

Railu wrenched the conversation back on its previous track: "You're right. Gherro would like her. No chance he found his way to her, I suppose." He shook his head, then turned to the percept. "I wanted to ask you if you couldn't help. Take a look in the crystal, the fire, whatever you use, and call his name. Gherro would surely answer a pretty woman that asked him nicely where the hell he was." Railu's smile was utterly disarming.

But the percept frowned. "I'm sorry. You have it wrong. I don't read thoughts or summon spirits by stone or fire. Nothing does my bidding, Knifedancer. The power . . . it's beyond my understanding or control. There is no way for me to seek out your friend."

"Something sent me here," Railu insisted. "Why else, if not to meet you?"

Lodvin was tapping the percept's shoulder. "Moabet, don't you think—"

She cut across his question with uncharacteristic abruptness. "Loddy, would you pour me some more moka? And I wonder if Cook made any more of those rolls?"

Stilpin chimed in, exclaiming about the time, and that set Vuorn to making his excuses, murmuring about work left undone. Within moments, half the breakfast party had gone their several ways. That left the percept and her lover facing Railu across the table.

"I meant what I said," Knifedancer told them. "It wasn't chance brought me here."

"Maybe you were led to us for another purpose than you think," Moabet suggested gently. She glanced from Railu to the door through which Chityr had gone. The faintest trace of a smile lit her face, lingering in her eyes. "Earlier, you mentioned something about wanting to find a different way of dancing to impress the people at that new inn. Why don't you talk to Loddy about it?''

Stilpin's expression lightened. She was fobbing Knife-dancer off on the maker. Loddy would talk his ear off, and leave nobody the worse for it.

Railu read that speaking look, but he paid more heed to the percept's expression. She had something up her sleeve —and nothing so ordinary as a knife. He rose with lazy grace. "Well then, I'll have to make do with that, won't I? Thank you, sera. Good morrow, ser." He strolled after Lodvin, amused at the odd turns this visit was taking. Perhaps the gods were just out for a bit of fun at his expense, but he was willing to play along.

When he found Lodvin (who had forgotten his errand already and stood in a courtyard behind the kitchen, watching a wandering beetle cross the flagstones), the maker disclaimed any ability to judge the merits of a dance. Railu delighted him by pulling out a few knives and giving an impromptu demonstration.

Lodvin responded with a shy smile. "I wonder if you'd care to see my new project. Nothing as grand as your talent, but I can't help thinking—well, I'll let you tell me if you see a use for it."

Railu grinned. "Lead on, friend." And went, all unknowing, to confront his destiny.

Stilpin paid the bearers and walked up the steps of Vuorn House, his shadow sharp in the moonlight. Sums, counter-offers, and the clauses of the final contract still rattled in his mind like the clicking beads of an abacus. But it was done. A third of Robellac's Xalycan holdings sold, in the utmost privacy, and the price paid in gold. Funds for engaging in the next fad to come, after the insanity of the relict trade— or profits to be stripped from the city if Xalycis fell to anarchy.

Stilpin grimaced at the thought of his own complicity, if Robellac plundered and ran.

With a hand lamp to light his way, Stilpin moved through the quiet house, his thoughts resuming their weary round. Robellac's loyalty resided in the traveling cities of his caravans. An agent-in-place was rootbound, unadventurous, just a jumped-up clerk. Like Moabet? Suddenly Stilpin was smiling, and his step quickened on the last flight of stairs. Almost home.

The room was empty, no sense of her presence. He gazed around him in a moment of irrational panic, then forced the fear back. Try the workrooms, the perfume chambers. Easy enough to lose track of the time with some experiment on hand. *Gods, 'Bet, don't have used the actives now!* You said you'd wait. . . .

Voices in the Great Chamber. Stilpin slipped in quietly. Lodvin Chityr and Moabet stood on either side of a shimmering mass, the height of a man. A conjured demon?

Chityr glanced at a small sand-glass. "Long enough. Try now. Can you move freely?"

As the apparition stirred, extending long, muscular arms, arching its back, it resolved into the figure of Railu Knifedancer, clad as the Glowing Man had been in nothing but a film of pigment. Not that outer skin of gold, though. Stretch, bend, turn, at every move the colors swirled and changed like spilt oil in a puddle, cloud gray, violet, scarlet. It took close scrutiny, with anger sharpening the eye, to see the man plain: hard buttocks, sinewy legs, one outthrust arm nearly brushing Moabet's shoulder.

Stilpin hurtled down to the stage and shoved him back. "Get away from her! What the hell are you playing at, Shandar?"

Moving with startling speed, Knifedancer whirled and dealt Stilpin a blow that, had it been in earnest, would have thrown him against the far wall instead of simply staggering him off his feet.

"It's the hero, come to rescue his fair maiden." Railu laughed, teeth white in a face of azure mottled with iridescent gold.

Lodvin, struck dumb by unexpected violence, gazed mutely from one young man to the other.

Then Moabet smartly slapped the dancer's face and went to kneel beside Stilpin. "Are you all right?"

Stilpin's sense of the absurd abruptly revived. He held out his hands, faintly luminous from their contact with the pigment. Moabet in turn displayed a brilliant palm. Then both looked up at Knifedancer. The fiery imprint of an open hand still marked his face. Stilpin laughed. "Well done, my lady!"

"But let's not make it part of the act, hey?" Railu rubbed his jaw. "Unless you're wild to take center stage at the Blue Lion."

Then Stilpin remembered the morning's talk of a new dance for the Wallwalk inn. They'd bought a consignment of surprisingly good wine just last week. "I wouldn't mind a visit to the Lion," he said. " 'Bet, shall I wangle an invitation?"

"Friends," Railu declared grandly, "you'll have the best seats in the house. My word on it." No matter that he'd not yet set foot in the Blue Lion or met its exotic master.

Stilpin tilted his head and scrutinized the dancer. "Make your own deals, do you? What will you ask above your standard fee, to dance on Wallwalk?"

"Above? Hell, a chance like this, you lose your first pay in kickbacks and you don't care." Railu scrubbed his face with a soaked towel provided by Lodvin. Rosy-tan skin emerged in streaks.

"That's a fool's game. The higher the price, the better the goods, that's how the buyer's mind works, once you've got his eye. Which d'you think the innmaster will respect—a two-orrin dancer or a fifty-orrin *performer*?"

"Like Mother," Lodvin put in, handing Railu another towel. "It's one of her favorite stories. When she was playing in *The Lost King*, Margola earned three hundred double-golds a day, enough to buy her own house."

"Three hundred. . . ." Railu drew in a breath. Then he sank to the floor beside Stilpin. "You think . . . ?"

Stilpin was thinking of the prices paid for relicts, and the eternal value of novelty. Remembering Knifedancer's ecstatic performance as Horse-Man in the Shandar sun rite. He gave a decisive nod. "One tenth-share to Lodvin for his pigment, one to me for handling the deal, 'Bet draws up the contract. I'll pay her clerk-fee." He gave the percept an unbusinesslike smile before turning back to Railu. "How about it?"

The knifedancer sprang up and into an iridescent cartwheel, followed by a back flip and an impudent Low Town waggle.

Lodvin gazed benignly. "Good comrades in partnership. Like something from an old tale, isn't it? We should clasp hands and swear loyalty to each other."

With only a little irony, they gathered together—gangling Lodvin, naked Knifedancer, Stilpin rumpled and weary-eyed, Moabet smiling like a wicked child.

Four hands met: Lodvin improvised a solemn oath.

Rodion of the Blue Lion stood on the parapet facing a sunset of a gaudy splendor rivaling his own magnificence. Gold cord bound his side-braided hair, and gold gleamed at neck and wrists. His beard, which had grown in gingery red, caught the sky's fire. A light wind rippled his tunic, sliding past the open throat, but could find no purchase on breeches smooth as a second skin. The blue-black sheen of his boots anticipated night.

Below him, a curving lane of raked gravel ran down through an avenue of wind-wracked trees to Wallwalk's clean, pale paving stones. He was twenty minutes' stroll from Arnix House and its neighbor Vuorn, had he conceived a desire to stray from his own domain. A kingdom of players! Gherifan felt a surge of delight. He had been ridiculously anxious when the trials began and the Blue Lion filled with Artists Vagabond. But none had recognized him in the man they sought to impress. Now the ultimate test would come. He had seen Knifedancer's name on the list of the evening's hopeful performers. Damn it, he'd hire him regardless, and the hell with prudence!

In the performers' waiting room, Stilpin stood beside Railu, feeling like a bodyguard to royalty. The Dancer had walked into the Blue Lion as though he owned it, ignoring his fellow applicants. The inn swarmed with them. Nervous actors seemed to pace in every room. Acrobats soberly limbered their muscles in hallways, like statuary come to life. Jangling jesters drew glares from musicians silently tracing the course of a new-learned melody. Friends—now rivals—avoided each other's eyes.

It was nearly midnight when Railu was finally called to the great stage in the theater that had been the ballroom of Nerra House. The air smelled of sweat, perfume, and tension. Stilpin sat in the small audience, his stomach a knot of ice.

"The Relict Dance, performed by Railu Knifedancer."

Screens slid back to reveal a single shaft of light, a dark hunched figure motionless within it. Gradually, the room grew still. In the high box where Rodion watched unseen, the low murmur of voices ceased.

Without benefit of accompaniment, relying solely on the spell of color and motion, Railu began to dance.

When it ended, a gaping message boy already stood before the stage. Awed by the dancer's glowing form, he managed to stammer out a summons from the master of the Blue Lion. Railu gave him a triumphant grin.

Clad in sweat-streaked pigment and a cotton robe, trailed by Stilpin (who had muttered a few instructions, then lapsed into taut, smiling silence), Railu went to his meeting with Rodion of Rhune.

The innmaster was alone, brilliantly clad as some exotic bird. He regarded his visitors levelly, but Stilpin caught a glint of humor in his eyes. Had the glory of the dance *amused* him?

"Please. Be seated. Admirably done, my gallant *ghe-Shandar*."

A western accent, right enough, and a manner florid as Master Robellac's. On the point of uttering some pleasantry about far travel, Stilpin was forestalled by Knifedancer's odd behavior. He knelt beside Rodion of Rhune, gripped the arms of his chair, and stared. Then he punched the innmaster's shoulder and collapsed backward, roaring with laughter. Had the pigment poisoned him, turned his brain? Dismayed, Stilpin started toward Rodion, and found him grinning like a boy caught in mischief.

"What did you do to him?" Stilpin demanded.

"Gave him a hint I thought he might need, the thick-head." The voice was pure Wallwalk. "I couldn't hire Dancer and keep him in ignorance. Great gods, he'd never forgive me."

Still shaky from his fit, Railu stood and crossed to a table set with wine. He upended the decanter over himself and began to wipe away the pigment with the sleeve of his robe. His features emerged, bearing an expression much like Rodion's. "You stinking son of a bitch." A selection of riper obscenities followed. All the while he was smiling. Finally, he clasped the innmaster in a bear hug. "Gherro!"

And Stilpin understood at last the absurd wonder of this reunion.

VII

Storm Crow

Jabel Fivesides warned Rodion to expect visitors before the Blue Lion officially opened its doors. Councilors and other public men would swarm like ants after spilled honey.

"Give 'em a taste, but not a handout," said the master of Masquer's Inn. "That's all been taken care of." He took a judicious sip of wine. Jabel, who knocked back common ale with the best of them at his own establishment, possessed a surprising knowledge of the finer vintages. This one seemed to meet with his approval. "So that's where the money goes," he grinned.

"Do I serve this stuff to the Council?" With Jabel, Rodion reverted to rough Leandric Gath, though the voice ill accorded with his present look, perfectly at ease in the outlandish clothes.

"Hell no, unless they're paying for it. But there's one always gets top service, no charge. Always." Jabel was dead serious now. "You give the Vinculine what he wants, no questions asked. Understand? Masquer's needs him, and the Lion too. Don't think he's got no clout in Hightown.''

Rodion did not think it. His Low City workers brought the news to Wallwalk: singers' tales, gossip, rumors whose wildest flights often proved to be plain truth. So he knew that Hendor Ebrin had addressed the Council, asking for funds to augment both his own guard and the Helm; that new laws were in force in Lowtown, harsh measures against relict thieves and dire punishments for public speakers who promoted unrest. Any High City man who overlooked the Vinculine's growing power did so at his peril. ''He gets the works, with bells on,'' Rodion agreed.

Jabel winked. ''Just keep Hendor happy.''

That evening, a sleek palanquin disgorged two councilmen, and with them the Vinculine. Rodion, alerted, was on the steps to greet them.

''Gentlemen! What a pleasure. Please, come in. The night air speaks of autumn. That pretty lady will take your cloaks. Would you care for some refreshment?'' Food, he silently hoped, for they were already well gone in drink.

Beneath the innmaster's pleasant chatter and unspoken concerns, Gherifan Arnix's heart beat faster—not simply for Jabel's advice on the handling of a man of power. The Vinculine had been at that fateful dinner when the seeress made her prophecy. Gherifan suspected it was Ebrin who had dined with the glass collector on the night he died. Was he an unwitting storm crow, flying before darkness—or was he something worse? Gherifan studied his distinguished guest. At Arnix House, Gherifan had avoided him; Hendor Ebrin always made him feel like a callow child. Now he looked at the Vinculine with the eyes of a man. Disarmingly ugly, energetic even in his cups, Ebrin was more vivid somehow than his companions. A small man larger than life.

Rodion quietly signaled to his servants. They brought an array of delicacies (with several bottles of the best wine) to one of the private card rooms: a sanctum where men might say or do anything, free from prying eyes.

Though the voice was slurred, the Vinculine's mocking wit remained agile. He told scurrilous anecdotes of absent councilors, to the delight of the present pair, lampooned his own efforts to govern Low Xalycis, and speculated on the habits of gaudy westerners in tight breeches—"present company always excepted." Rodion laughed with the rest. Deep in his thoughts lay the bloodstained room, the immense absence of Aubric i-Arnix. Mistrust rose, to be turned away by an irresistible tale of feuding stall keepers, a lecherous lampman, or the sexual quirks of the Commander of the Helm. This was the talk he had missed, self-exiled from his father's table. Now the great men came to him.

After the meal, they began a haphazard round of cards. At a councilman's urging, three of the inn's women were brought. Gherifan's attention sharpened. Jabel had taught him how a man revealed himself in his dealings with women, cruel or doting, indifferent or obsessed. The older councilman seemed content to fondle bare breasts and "teach" his partner a game of chance she knew better than he. The younger, from one of the Walk's wealthiest families, began to sprinkle his talk with blunt obscenities, one eye on the smiling lady of his choice. And the Vinculine? He won a considerable sum at cards, watched with pleasure as the third courtesan removed her clothes, then presented her to the innmaster with a light smack on her bottom.

"Come, Master Rodion, enjoy your own stock. You've surely earned it."

"What of yourself, ser?" So long-legged Thera didn't catch his fancy? Most short men liked them tall.

A sweeping gesture. "I prefer the role of benefactor."

Thera ran her hands down her employer's chest and began to unlace his shirt, grinning at him. Balanced between arousal and annoyance, Gherifan caught the Vinculine's eye, and realized he was under the amused scrutiny of the man whose measure he had meant to take. A clever man twice his age.

Though his pulse throbbed uncomfortably, Gherifan managed to disengage himself with a laugh and an easy jest. Thera curled in a chair and watched as innmaster and Vinculine took up the cards again. When the game was done, the Vinculine casually cast his winnings over her in a glittering shower.

Weeks of careful preparation collapsed into a muddle of last-minute emergencies on the day of the opening gala. Rodion had no time to oversee the performers' final rehearsals. They would have to suffer their last crises of nerves without reassurance from the innmaster. His own nerves were in a bad enough state.

He winced every time he encountered one of the new guards. That morning, Mog had brought a squad of Jabel's more presentable toughs along with word that some dream-peddler named Sandhound might be coming in after his lost maker. Never mind why Hound thought the man was here: what would he try to *do* about it?

Then there was the Vinculine's woman. Ebrin's response to a formal invitation to the post-gala dinner had included the scrawled afterthought, "and Jesimis-nenna." They had been quarreling in public. Would she make a scene tonight? Gherifan remembered how betrayed he had felt, an idealistic boy shocked when his neighbor Vuorn's beautiful wife fled Wall-walk with her lover. Now he felt a stab of pity.

"Innmaster? There's a potboy burnt himself at an oven yelling his head off and Cook's about to throw a fit."

"Innmaster—what do I do with twelve bales of yellow

velvet the carter just left at the gate? Nobody told me about any yellow velvet.''

The simultaneous arrival of these supplicants drove the thoughts of Sandhound and Jesimis out of Rodion's head. There were problems enough closer to hand.

An hour after moonrise, the Blue Lion's lower rooms were packed, and still the palanquins came. The inn had been invaded by a brilliant, chattering flock, atwitter over the transformation of Nerra House into this upstart establishment. They could find little fault with it. The Blue Lion gleamed with the fine gloss of money shrewdly spent, elegant as in old Nerra's heyday, with just a hint of riper pleasures to be had somewhere discreetly out of sight. As for Rodion of Rhune, who had ever seen such clothes (cloth of gold tonight, with violet piping and diamonds at throat and wrists)? Or such manners? He greeted each group of new arrivals with the same flamboyant courtesy, yet his poise bespoke arrogance as if the rumors might be true that he was a prince in exile. In his wake, men fingered their conventionally beardless chins while women plied their fans in a wild flutter of painted silk. Rodion remained the undisputed center of attention until the belated arrival of the Vinculine's party.

Stolid bodyguards cleared the way before them. Rodion had room enough to perform his most elaborate bow. ''Vinculine. This is an extraordinary honor.'' He straightened, to encounter Ebrin's amused regard and the dark stare of the woman at the Vinculine's side. She was thinner than Gherifan remembered her. Long fingers lay pale against her cloak's opulent brocade, black as her hair. Ebrin made no move to introduce Jesimis-nenna, but let her notoriety stand sufficient in itself.

''Innmaster. How good to see you again.'' The Vinculine rested a hand on his mistress's shoulder. When she remained silent, he cast her a glance of exaggerated forbearance. "The Raven is shy tonight. Perhaps your magnificence overawes her." With a twitch of his fingers, he sent the cloak cascading to the floor. The gown beneath was virginal white—and lewd as a whore's caress. Her least movement teased the eye with a glimpse of thigh, hip, breasts, through slits in the pleated gauze. Every man in the room would mentally strip her bare. Only her chilling gaze might deter them, if they made the mistake of meeting it.

Rodion met it head-on. "Sera. You honor us."

A flicker of rage in the dark eyes gave way to some more complex emotion as she realized he spoke sincerely. Still, she did not answer.

"Forgotten her party manners," the Vinculine said with a laugh. "Silly girl." He smiled at Rodion. "I give her to you, Innmaster—for this one night. A small token of my esteem."

Gherifan nearly burst through Rodion's glittering shell to seize Hendor Ebrin by the throat. Jesimis forestalled him. Moving with the assurance of a queen robed in majesty, she paced toward the innmaster and took his arm. "Shall we go in, ser, to the entertainments?" Her voice was low, throaty. Raised in anger, it would crack. At the moment it was under tight control. "We mustn't keep the others waiting."

Ebrin watched this tableau, still smiling. *Last time I wouldn't rise to his bait,* Gherifan realized with a degree of awe at the man's effrontery. *So he takes his revenge on both of us, rejected mistress and upstart innmaster.*

The innmaster's face remained blank for a moment, then blossomed into a grin that would have looked well on a Tumbleside cutthroat—or a barbarian prince. "Sera, your word is my will."

"Good fortune, Innmaster." Ebrin gave an ironic salute, then moved into the miraculously parting crowd, guards alert on either flank and a third at his back.

Rodion had time for one last wayward thought before he turned to follow, Jesimis-nenna on his arm. *Knifedancer, you've got your work cut out to top the opening act. . . .*

Railu Knifedancer stood alone in darkness on the stage, his body black with cold pigment. He waited, breathing shallowly, listening to the sounds of the crowd, that great, murmurous creature waiting in its turn for him. The last lights dimmed.

A sidelong radiance crept toward him, and a bell-tree shivered. For a moment he remained motionless, shadow against deeper shadow. Then one arm drifted from his side, to the pure, sweet ringing of a single bell. The closed palm opened: scarlet shading into blue, a hovering witchfire.

Flute and drum and bells sounded together, and seemed to call the dancer to life, color blossoming from forearm to shoulder, a swirl of palest green-gold spilling across the arched back, ice and azure along one outstretched leg, the muscles taut. A spinning turn, as the drumbeat quickened, and the witchfire flared, lingering in the eye moments after the dancer had moved on. Phantom blurs and smears of color filled the stage.

He dropped to a crouch, arms stiffly bent. The flute began a low, sinuous music that wrapped him round, made the shining figure sway, the poised mass begin to flow like molten glass, collapsing in on itself. Somber drums, a whispering gong. The music stuttered to a halt, resumed and shifted rhythms, as the darkness yielded up new whorls and skeins of light, and the colors crawled. A haze of emerald overlaying violet suddenly thrust outward, for an instant clear, the form of a leaping man, then tumbling back into chaos.

When Railu flung himself down again, hearing his heartbeat louder than the drums, the shifting pigment slid through changing hues all on its own, dancing across his flesh as he lay still through one full measure. In the hall, men of consequence forgot the tally of their wealth. Elders no longer grimaced at the music's strangeness. Watchers who had sought the naked flesh beneath the paint gazed in a dream, beyond desire. Sophisticates unmoved by the previous efforts of singer and jester lost their indifference in a rush of wonder. Wallwalk's haughtiest aristos gaped like children.

As the dance reached its whirling, dazzling climax, innmaster Rodion and Jesimis-nenna stood close together in a hidden alcove and stared with the same rapt delight, unaware that their hands touched. In his guarded box, the Vinculine sat rigid, almost free in that moment from his own hungry soul.

The Relict Dance ended with a falling shadow, one last flicker of blue flame, and silence. A sigh rustled through the hall as men and women released pent breath. Applause began as a pattering off to one side, then spread, gathered force, became a rhythmic pounding under the roar of voices joined in a continuous shout.

Railu had already slipped from the stage in a hooded cloak, following Stilpin's advice: "No bows, no encores. Leave them with the mystery."

When Stilpin and Dalu came to the dressing room, they found a strangely diminished figure with sweat-soaked hair and dulled green eyes, rubbing off the pigment with a smeared towel.

This once, the chemic had no gruff words for his grandnephew. Dalu laid one hand on the damp, hard-muscled shoulder. "That was rightly done."

Railu's great smile appeared at last. Then, glancing away almost shyly, he murmured a Shandar phrase of thanks for god-grace.

Outside, the clamor had finally died away. Stilpin went to the door. The backstage was still clear of visitors, and he hoped Rodion's men could carry out their orders to keep out even the most distinguished guests. A sudden image of the Vinculine striding in and coming face-to-face with Dalu sent a shiver up his spine. Though the chemic never spoke directly of the man who had taken Vuorn's wife, Stilpin knew Dalu would not forgive that offense against honor.

He was roused from his thoughts by muffled shouts, their direction uncertain. "Something's happening."

Railu joined him. "They're after a gate-crasher, sounds like." Swiftly he scrambled into his clothes, and returned to the doorway with a knife ready in his hand.

"Want to go look?" Stilpin spoke with an offhand bravado that he scarcely felt.

"It'll come to us." Head cocked, Railu listened to noises familiar from Low City brawls and vendettas, the thud of running boots—louder now, pursuers like a herd of bulls.

They ran down their prey at the far end of the space behind the stage. Amid the knot of men, something shone the yellow of old bone. Stilpin's hands clenched and he swore. "Sandhound. He must be crazy, coming here." In the crowd, a fist rose and fell. The figure in pale leather staggered under the blow. They could see him clearly now, bent with his hands to his knees. Sandhound straightened, shaking his head as if dazed. Then the scene exploded as men were flung back from its center, where the intruder whirled with a metal rod blurring around him. Blood sprayed where he'd scored a hit.

"I didn't think he was such a brawler." Stilpin winced in sympathy as another blow connected.

"Looks like those boys need some help." Railu shoved the knife in his belt and began to roll up his sleeves.

"No you don't, boy. One step farther, I'll have your hide." Dalu plucked the weapon away, stowing it in his own shapeless tunic. "Sandhound's run wild on one of his smokes, wouldn't feel a blade if it went clear through him. You can get that precious face of yours bashed in some other night.''

Reflexively, the dancer rubbed his nose. "Doesn't seem right, standing by."

"Hell, it's six against one," Stilpin put in. "There, they've almost—he's down. Unless you want to rescue him?"

Railu grinned. "I don't think our friend would thank me."

"With a foot of steel in your guts," Dalu muttered.

Sandhound was shouting for Lodvin Chityr, a jumble of threats and bribes silenced only by a blow to the head that rocked him off balance.

A door banged back. Innmaster Rodion strode in, set-faced and ominously silent until he reached the cluster of men. "Who is this?"

"A mad dog," someone offered, provoking laughter quickly stilled by Rodion's cool stare.

"Name of Sandhound," a second man put in.

The stare focused on the prisoner. "Got past you at the doors, did he? So much for our prized security. Someone had better go for the Helm. He's their business now." Rodion continued to regard the dazed figure hanging limp between two of Jabel's brawlers. The detachment in his voice acted like a whipcrack, setting a message-bearer into motion as the others straightened self-consciously.

But the messenger was stopped before he could reach the door.

"That won't be necessary." Flanked by his own guards, the Vinculine emerged from the shadows. "How would your Hightown patrons take it to find Lowtown intruding here, right at their own doorsteps . . . attracted by this experiment of Jabel's, it would seem. *Associated* in some way with your splendid dancer. What a pity, if wild rumors spoiled your well-deserved triumph, Master Rodion." His glance flicked from master to prisoner and back. "I can deal with the vermin for you. A favor to a friend."

Watching, Dalu grunted. "Like calls to like." He kept a grip on Railu's arm—tense with the dancer's anger.

Railu was swearing under his breath. "If he comes in here, I'll rip out his liver. 'Associated'!" Then a movement in the doorway behind the innmaster distracted him. "Would you look at that!"

Jesimis-nenna joined the group around Sandhound, making her way to the Vinculine's side. "Another creature for your menagerie, Hendor? Haven't you enough of them already?"

The Vinculine began to sing in a pleasant tenor, "A raven and a hound have I/Masters of blood and bone/On fields of battle they shall dine/And never sup alone." He slipped an arm around her waist. "My sweet, do you confuse me with King Death in the old play?" Casually he bestowed a more intimate caress.

Two of Rodion's men snickered. The innmaster himself had an expression oddly similar to Jesimis's, as if both had donned the same rigid mask. Yet his voice was easy enough as he turned to the Vinculine and said, "If you're after sport, Excellence, it's on the house. The ladies would be honored."

From his vantage at the door, Railu could not read the Vinculine's heavy features, but he grinned and murmured, "Ah, Ser Vinculine, what to do? Choose the Raven, the Hound, or Rodion's sweet Hell?"

"But I am absurdly forgetful!" Ebrin cried. "The lady is not mine again until the sun rises. Indeed, I must ease my spirits as the innmaster so hospitably suggested."

"What about this 'un?" one of the inn's guards asked with wrinkling brow and a tip of the head toward Sandhound.

"He'll keep." The Vinculine directed his guards to bind and gag the prisoner. Then he favored Jabel's men with a wink. "Or he can come along and watch."

* * *

Since the first night of the Relict Dance, the Blue Lion had become a Wallwalk fashion, as absorbing to its most fervent devotees as the pursuit of relicts was to diggers in the Tumbles, as costly to some as an appetite for *calasta* or *khur*. A few came even by day, to gamble in windowless rooms where lamps continually burned. Others mingled with the crowds who arrived for each night's entertainment, but Gherifan learned to pick them out, the passionate ones who held back hour upon hour before going to the women, the nonchalant observers whose eyes turned rapt and hungry upon one special performer. On Railu Knifedancer above all, those days when he appeared and—rare delight—walked among them. Railu joked that he'd marry the richest of them, "man or woman," though he soon found ways to detach himself from the most ardent.

To the dancer's amusement, Innmaster Rodion also had admirers. Flowers from the choicest Wallwalk gardens mysteriously accumulated before his door, some of them twined with gold or braided pearls. The inn might have swarmed with hirsute imitators as well, if Jabel Fivesides hadn't placed a ban on visitors with side braids and pointed beards, "unless they be true westerners." To Gherifan's relief, no travelers from the West appeared.

Nor did the Vinculine return to the Blue Lion. Rumor had him in a dozen places: breaking up a secret cult of relict-worshipers, wringing dark secrets from Sandhound, writing a philosophy of government, consulting with oracles, scholars, priests. The limits of his office seemed to drift wider with each day. It was only a matter of time before the Council must bow to it and agree that in this new era of the Artifact, Xalycis could have only one master.

Each dawn Gherifan stripped off his glittering costume and lay open-eyed in bed, thinking of the dead, of Aubric i-Arnix and plundered relicts, of the glass collector and his bitter widow. They were the only truths that did not shift with the changes from Gherifan to Gath, Gath to Rodion, Rodion to the nameless man with his head on swans-down pillows and no peace in his heart.

One morning, a little after dawn, he heard a scratching at the hall door. He was on his feet and halfway through the outer office before he wondered what he could do, naked and weaponless, against a determined intruder. Wait . . . yes, gods be thanked, he'd left one ornamental dagger on the desk near the glass lion. Careful to make no sound, he unsheathed the blade, tested the edge. It would have to serve.

The door clicked open. A dark, cloaked figure, face blurred behind a wind scarf, slipped in, quietly shut the door, and crossed to the window. Gherifan had retreated to the inner doorway where he watched, unseen.

A rustle of silk, the creak of a shutter that needed oiling, and suddenly the room was filled with pale light.

Pulling off her wind scarf, she turned and saw him. "Innmaster. Forgive my informality, and the early hour of this visit. I had no choice."

Not a would-be murderer or thief. Nor an amorous admirer—the husky voice was cool, contained. The sunlight revealed lines around her eyes that he had not seen at their first meeting, and it hollowed her face with shadows like bruises under the sharp cheekbones. Jesimis-nenna, the Vinculine's woman.

"What do you want?" he asked.

She surveyed him, lips quirking a little. "Not what the circumstances might suggest. I'm told you have a glass ornament for which you named this inn. Might I see it?"

Gherifan gestured with the hand not holding the dagger. "The display case on the desk."

The light had not yet penetrated to that side of the room,

or she would have spotted it at once, burning blue. Jesimis-nenna bent over the case, then lifted it carefully and brought it to a table nearer the window. For a long moment she gazed. Finally, "It's true, then. You have one of them. Come and see another." From a pocket in her cloak she drew a lacquered box. As Gherifan approached, setting the dagger aside on his way, she removed the raw cotton padding around a velvet pouch that held something that gleamed darkly. It was a winged serpent fashioned from black glass. Where the sun struck the half-open wings they glowed red-brown, and tendrils on the serpent's head were a smoldering crimson. The coiled body resisted light, reducing it to an icy sheen over shadow.

There could be no doubt. This was one of the pieces the widow had described, stolen on the night of her husband's murder.

"Ebrin gave you this?"

"Yes. There are more. Quite a ceremony he made of presenting them, trophies of manhood. Making sure I knew he'd stolen them. That was the fun of it, he thought, being beyond suspicion or pursuit." A mirthless smile.

"The man who owned them was murdered on the night of the theft. His widow gave me the lion because she couldn't bear to look at it for the memories." Gherifan stood at the table, staring down at the two small masterworks that had once belonged to Murn.

"Murdered?" That startled her.

"Did you think he was merely a thief?" Gherifan shook his head, the unbound hair flowing across his shoulders. "No, madam. You underestimate the Vinculine."

Jesimis seized his forearm and gazed fiercely into his eyes. "Who are you? How do you know these things? Don't try to tell me you're plain Rodion of Rhune, far from home. You've no more accent than I have."

Oddly, that was the greater nakedness. He had not been Rodion, had lost him somewhere, and the shield of his presence was gone. He felt the blood rise in his face. "Gherifan Arnix," he blurted. "I think—I'm sure—he killed my father too."

She released him as though burned. "Pitiless gods." Finding the chair behind her, she sank down, closed her eyes.

"You must have suspected." Gaining confidence, he leaned toward her, hands resting flat on the table on either side of the lion and the serpent. "You can't have lived with him, *slept* with him, and not known."

Jesimis made a sound somewhere between a chuckle and a sob. "My dear boy, copulation has never been the path to knowledge. The opposite, if anything. Your courtesans could tell you that it's commerce clears the mind. Not lust, not love."

"You loved him?"

A shrug that might indicate self-contempt or a hard-won indifference. Then the brittle elegance vanished from her pose, and the low voice softened. "Gherifan Arnix. You climbed the wall into Vuorn's garden. I used to walk there every day, but you could have spied on me for weeks, I wouldn't have noticed. It must have provoked you to be so disregarded. One day you tossed a stone at me. A sturdy, silk-haired child."

"I was twelve," he replied hotly. "And it would have been flowers, but they were too light to clear the wall."

"Flowers?" She smiled.

"You looked so unhappy."

"Oh, I was—and loving every minute of it." Her smile twisted with self-mockery. "Misery is one of life's subtler pleasures."

He frowned down at her. "That's what the drunkards tell me as they weep over their wine. I hear it every night, how subtle and sad they all think they are, till the cold sweats come and they stagger out to vomit."

"Appalling, isn't it? Human weakness." Jesimis laughed —the Raven's croak.

Gherifan seized her by the shoulders. "Why did you come here?"

She gazed at him steadily. "I don't know. A whim, a brainstorm. Perhaps a deathwish, though I had no knowledge of his killings. I've left him."

"And he let you go?"

"Hendor has become careless of late. There is much on his mind. Do you think I'm a danger to him now?" Her voice broke on the question, not from anger or fear but from surprise. He was staring at her with the oddest expression; it might almost have been tenderness. She echoed his own question. "Why are you here, Innmaster Rodion?"

"For you. To meet you, learn what you know, and encompass our revenge." The stern words were accompanied by feather-light touches of his hand, like a caress of wind against her cheek, her brow, her lips.

She rose from the chair. They were of a height. And they faced each other with the same look, at once hungry and wryly self-aware. The boy in the garden was a man grown.

VIII

Black *Khur*

From the notebooks of Lodvin Chityr:

Moabet rarely writes anything down. All the world fits into her head and is brought to order there. But I'm a man of the pen like my father before me. I must write or things slide away. She has looked at all my notes on the active essences—praised them too, sweet girl. Few of the actives I made for Sand-hound will suit her purpose. Her thoughts race without benefit of *alal*, and she loves more deeply than *calasta* could ensure. Last night we tried snakeweed (or she did; she insisted I wear a filter mask like Stilpin's). The part of her mind she calls the "flaw" was teased half to waking—not enough. I've flown on higher doses, but her body mass is too small to handle what Loddy the gawk can manage. Stilpin watches her as though she might evaporate on the next breeze. She is not so fragile as that.

[There follows a series of calculations involving

dosages of red *khur*. These give way to a compressed account of another experimental session, ending with an abrupt slash of the pen and the scrawled words, "So close I could weep! It's to be the black then, as we knew all along."]

Vuorn lay awake, listening to the distant sound of the fans turning in one of his perfume chambers. Moabet, Stilpin, and their renegade chemic. He knew what they did there. Moabet had as good as confessed it yesterday, without needing to say a word. They had come to a mute understanding. Stilpin, though, had a hangdog, haggard look. Vuorn must speak to him, tell him the time was ripe for heresy and rebellion. Let the fans turn and the air blow strange and new through these old halls!

Brave words. Beneath them lay fear like a stone bound to his heart. Fascination, repulsion, the itch of curiosity: The cycle of emotions ran its round. Might they value an older man's accumulated experience? Could he bear to meddle with the forbidden? How could he stay away?

At last he sighed, rose from his bed, and threw on a plain cotton robe. Etroren i-Vuorn walked through his ancestral home, letting its silence calm his thoughts. The marble stairway had been hollowed by countless footsteps—all history and high lineage reduced to a slow wearing away of stone. On other sleepless nights that image had disturbed him, as though he moved through the cold magnificence of his own tomb, last of the family Vuorn. Now the familiar tilts and troughs beneath his bare feet felt like a part of himself. He wore the house like a garment, a second skin.

Vuorn hesitated for a moment at the perfume chamber's outer door. Then he gave a gentlemanly knock. Stilpin answered, face mask slung around his neck. His eyes looked bruised with worry and fatigue. "Etroren. . . ."

"I thought I could assist," Vuorn said. "Which active do you try tonight?"

Rubbing a stubbled jaw, Stilpin could not meet the master perfumer's eyes. "Black *khur*."

Vuorn drew in a breath and felt his heartbeat speed. With an effort, he achieved a semblance of cool interest. "I should like to see the test if it still goes on. Will you indulge my curiosity?"

Stilpin ducked his head in mute acknowledgment. Then he regained the power of speech. "I'll get you a mask and tell Loddy. We're between trials. Different dilutions. Wait here a moment."

Vuorn entered the anteroom as Stilpin fled through the inner door. When Stilpin returned, an extra filter mask in his hand, he looked calmer. "Loddy'd be glad of your help." The smile was nearly genuine. "Thank you."

Entering the perfume chamber, Vuorn quickly slipped on the mask. Lodvin appeared to be ready for the next trial, a perfume wand charged with dilute *khur* resting on the table before him. Moabet sat in a high-backed chair, hands resting lightly on its arms. Stilpin was cross-legged on the floor at her feet, nose and mouth covered by his mask. It looked like a tableau from some strange Low City cult. Vuorn took over the manipulation of the fans from Lodvin with a bare exchange of words. Then Lodvin raised the wand.

Invisibly, the dilute *khur* spread through the chamber. Vuorn found himself holding his breath. Pointless, unless the mask failed. He forced himself to breathe evenly and keep a light touch on the cords. Lodvin moved the perfume wand with a delicate exactitude, where Vuorn had expected wild swoops.

Moabet seemed to have entered the first stage of a trance: relaxed, eyelids lowered, her breathing slow but regular.

"What do you see, 'Bet?" Stilpin asked. "Where do you walk?"

She replied so softly he had to lean toward her to catch the words.

Vuorn's brows rose, but he did not risk breaking in with a question. Moabet was murmuring something more.

Stilpin placed his hands over hers and stared into her tranced face. "Are you sure?"

Evidently she was. He stood, frowning. "Loddy, she's remembering the bonereader's place. There was a residue of smoke from a reading by black *khur*—gods know how long before, but . . ." He cut off the thought with a glum shrug. "She says the *khur* must be burnt. Something about impurities."

Lodvin and Vuorn gave the same nod of comprehension. The perfume art purified, stylized, made even the active essences elegant. Sometimes the truth was more crude. Makers knew it; perfumers had their suspicions. Without a word exchanged, Vuorn set the fans to sweep away the last trace of dilute *khur*, and Lodvin began to pack up his materials.

"Is there enough left for burning?" Stilpin asked.

"Oh, yes. They gave us a great deal—all their stock, perhaps." Lodvin grinned. "The benefit of divine intervention."

Vuorn would have liked to have probed into this odd statement (just how had they met Chityr?), but the percept was beginning to rouse.

Stilpin turned to her immediately, pulling down his filter mask. " 'Bet?"

"I'm all right. A little tired." She smiled at him.

He drew her into a close embrace. The movement of the fans ruffled their hair as though they stood on a windy clifftop, lovers reunited at the Caravan Gate after long parting. Vuorn could almost feel the giddy sweep of distance around them.

* * *

Vuorn stopped the experiments for a day. He wanted no trace of dilute *khur* lingering in the percept's body when they tried the essence again, and they all needed sleep. None for himself, of course. He wanted to bring Dalu Chemic into this, and it might take some hard talking to win the Shandar over. Dalu was home in Ladder Valley; Vuorn would go to him. Unaware of his servants' astonishment, he ordered a palanquin.

A strange day in Vuorn House, with the shutters closed as if a sand wind raged (the sky was flawless blue), and the guests lying in their beds while the master went off on his own for the first time in years. Scandalous goings-on—and wonderful. Maybe the old place was coming back to life at last. The household staff tiptoed. It was a holiday for Maiga, the upstairs maid. No bedrooms to clean, except the master's, and no new tasks set her. She found a patch of sun slanting through a skylight onto the stairs and sat to bask for a moment. Despite the warmth, she went a bit shivery when she thought of the percept sleeping up there after gods knew what witchery.

Maiga's head was drooping when a cry from above roused her. She scrambled to her feet and ran back up to the corridor. Which room? The percept's—of course. When no one answered her knock, she opened the door a timid crack and peeped in. Then closed it hastily.

"All right, Maiga. I'm decent." Stilpin's voice sounded odd, hollow like the heart had gone out of him. "Please come help me."

"What can I do?" She was into the room before she saw the percept and gasped.

"Another fit," he said grimly. He had wrapped Moabet in all the covers when he woke to her cry and found her shivering, tranced, skin icy to the touch. Now she looked unsettlingly like a corpse. "Maiga—" His air of resolve abruptly cracked. "I don't know what to do. This isn't like before."

Maiga took a hesitant step closer. "She's going to prophesy?"

"I think so." He scrubbed a hand through his tousled hair. "It *feels* like she will, if that makes any sense. But it's trapped somehow."

"Ask her a question." That's how the street-corner prophets did it anyway.

"Brilliant, Maiga!" He flustered her with a kiss on the cheek, then turned to the bed. Gently he stroked Moabet's brow. " 'Bet. Can you hear me?"

The percept's eyes opened. Sightless.

"Come on, love," he urged. "*Moabet*. Tell me what you see."

No answer. Her head was tilted away from him, as though someone sat at her other side and spoke to her.

"What do you hear?"

This drew a response at last. She spoke in the strange slow voice of a dreamer. "He calls. He cries. He wants. . . . Alone so long. They are lonely. Locked in the skull-egg."

This baffling speech ended with a restless movement. She almost seemed to wake.

" 'Bet, sweet love, are you—?"

Moabet did not turn to him as he had hoped. Still the spell held her. But when she spoke again, her tone was radically different: a percept riding the flood tide of observation. "The globe is smooth—no, it seems so, because of the shining. Something moves inside. Trapped. Skeins and coils and knots. How did they—? No time for that." A slight headshake. "It exists in sequence, room within room like nested boxes. Beneath a high dome. A vague place next. Hard to see. Then a vault. Arnix House." She grimaced. "Crippled things. Blood." Moabet began to shiver again.

Stilpin wrapped his arms around her. "All right, love. That's over. Done with."

"No!" she cried. "They need to speak. He's so alone. Help me. . . ."

"Where are you now?" It was the crucial question, but she gave no answer. Stilpin drew back a little and anxiously scanned her face. Pale and expressionless, a blank mask—like that smooth globe she had been talking about. The Artifact. And within it a living mind.

"Trapped one. Tell me your name. Your *name*," he commanded.

Her lips moved to form a word in silence.

"Aloud!"

This time, the answer came clearly, each syllable pronounced with cold precision: "Ar-khen-az-u-ril."

Down the percept's face ran two slow drops of blood. Then she slumped unconscious, still bleeding from the nostrils.

Maiga, who had gaped in uncomprehending horror during the questioning, fled to get help. She returned with a sleep-rumpled Lodvin. The maker quickly took charge. In moments, Maiga was fussing over Moabet with extra pillows and warm towels, like a midwife at some strange birthing. Lodvin drew Stilpin aside.

"She'll be fine. Don't worry about the bleeding. A bit of excitement, that's all."

"It's the damned black *khur*—killing her."

"No. Not at all." Lodvin plucked at his sleeve. "Come with me and listen."

When Vuorn returned with Dalu Chemic, Moabet lay in peaceful sleep, Lodvin fizzed with speculations, and Stilpin sat dazed after a long session mixing reassurances and sharp debate. Loddy had more than held his own in argument. Stilpin had no defenses against his brilliance. Now one thought filled Stilpin's mind: He could not stop them. The experiments would go on, would roll right over him if he stood in their way. Just look at Vuorn and the chemic, listening to Lodvin tell his tale. They were fascinated, caught in the lure of the Artifact as surely as Arnix had been, and entranced with the mysteries of *khur*.

The Greater Perfume Chamber was transformed into a bonereader's lair—shadowy, filled with thin smoke and an unsettling sense of presences hovering unseen or on the edge of vision. Dalu presided over the brazier where the black *khur* smoldered. Lodvin sat bolt upright with his notebook in his lap, clutching a pen so tightly it was in danger of snapping clean in two. Vuorn paced the stage, unused to having idle hands—they had decided to leave the fans at rest until the end. Stilpin brooded beyond the reach of the light. All of the men wore filter masks. Only Moabet remained vulnerable to the power of the smoke.

Gingerly, Dalu placed a second lump of black *khur* on the coals. He missed the solemn ceremony of a Shandar rite, but who could dictate the ritual of this deed? Not the mad cultists, the dog-killers in the Tumbles. Nor the adepts of Bonereaders Court. For all their privileged access to the dead, they could not encompass such a wonder as the Artifact, miraculously alive.

Moabet's head sank back against the tall, cushioned chair, and her hands relaxed. Vuorn stopped his pacing, quietly took a seat.

After a long moment, Dalu broke the silence. "Moabet Shar. Has your journey begun?"

The wind spoke with his voice in the wasteland where the trance had taken her, rousing Moabet from contemplation of an infinite line of broken pillars receding under a night sky.

"I'm here," she answered. But it was time to see where the ancient road might take her. . . . No! The thought roused her to new alertness. The road extended at her bidding, and would bring her wherever she wished to go.

She had eluded the first trap of black *khur*. The next was worse, for how should she choose, with all the world and the immensities of time opening out, awaiting her? The far, far past was a vertiginous gulf that drew her to its brink, a lure of beginnings, ultimate things, all questions laid to rest in a single answer. Moabet shivered and stepped back. That way lay death.

Out, then, into the kingdoms of man? Patterns lay beneath the chaos of history. She could trace them, see their weaving, unbind the threads to find the warp beneath. Almost she felt her fingers on the great, dark loom. Unraveler. Weaver of the world's fate.

"To work, girl. Where are your wits?" The mask muffled Dalu's words, as though he were a mumbling ancient. Would she hear—and smite him for his presumption? He sensed the power that had entered her with the thin smoke.

The wind sent her hair tumbling. Grown back nearly to her shoulders now, it was the only part of her not cold with a tense readiness like ice beneath the skin. Moabet stepped forward onto a narrow path whose borders towered into darkness, closing her in even as she ran freely down its length.

And then she was among the ghosts of masonry and glimmering plaster, skeletal lath, a curving in the air where tiles had risen or would rise to shield the buildings of the city. Xalycis of the mages, its very paving stones bright with their glamor and hard-won dominion; Xalycis aflame, a scramble of greed through the ruins; renewal, survival, walls standing tall again amid forgotten balefires, dimming histories of loss. Smoke stung her nostrils, sharp as fresh-spilled blood. Did she seek for pattern? Here it was, brutally clear. Recurrence: for every builder a breaker, for each miracle of healing, artistry, united purpose, a devil's laughter at the frailty of man's endeavors. Gleeful gathering and squandering, a smoking desolation.

Despair is the third trap in the realm of black *khur*. The wind-voice countered it with a name. "Arkhenazuril."

So swiftly the phantom city blurred and shifted around her, she was dizzied, shaken from her sense of self. Fighting vertigo, she concentrated on the wind's cool touch.

"Arkhenazuril buried in earth. Lost. Forgotten. You I awaken." Ah, clever voice. The force within the Artifact might be weaker, more amenable, if she reached it before its rediscovery.

Silence. A third time the voice invoked it, a priest coaxing an obstinate god.

Like a spill of fine soil before the land cracks wide, the first words came: "Arrive. Heart. Here." And then, as some barrier collapsed: "The time the slow and silver range where—where he is walking beside the wall, we are side-climbing through beauty of the stone the swift and—blind, the hawks caught his eyes, hot, the burning star, staring it flows, it—"

The manic ranting seemed unstoppable. Prophet, bard, or mage, the creature in the Artifact occupied some region beyond sane discourse.

"Feeding the rain. *Feeding* the *rain*. Listen, listen, listen. . . ."

Moabet broke the link—or pulled away, for she could still sense the mad mind crying from its prison. It was a triumph to have this much control over the vision, to be aware, alert. And yet she nearly wept from disappointment. Whatever Arkhenazuril had been, it had become no better than a relict now, randomly lurching between pattern and chaos. Unless something in the *khur*, or in her own imperfect mind, had driven it out of control? A new thought chilled her. The results of her tampering might be manifest to the Artifact's new possessor—Arnix's murderer.

She restored contact, then tried to see around her through whatever might pass for the Artifact's senses. There was someone in the room. Asleep. Ill? A wrongness somewhere . . . a pinpoint of light glittering in the palm of one pale hand. Moabet flinched from the vision as if scalded, and was back in the perfume chamber. It spun, then steadied. Stilpin slipped a filter mask over her head, anxiously watching her. Dalu had already doused the *khur*. Though her heart still pounded with a remnant of the fear, Moabet's curiosity was coming into play. Who had she seen? What was the horror in that tiny fleck of blue? She was determined to find out.

"Don't you want to find her—teach her she can't run off like that?"

"Raven? She can make her own way to hell."

"She was mine, I'd track her down and cut her." Sandhound's pale eyes narrowed a little as he smiled. "Doesn't take much to change a woman's looks."

"Leave it, Hound." The Vinculine seemed bored, scarcely attending to the conversation.

"A man should hold on to what's his," Sandhound persisted.

"Tell that to Aubric i-Arnix. He lost more than a tedious woman, didn't he?" Ebrin's gaze rested blandly upon Hound.

Who frowned, then got the joke. "Guess he just had slippery fingers, that old man Arnix."

"After I was through with him, he did." The Vinculine grinned and settled back more comfortably in his chair.

Hound could be a nuisance, with his harping on vengeance and old wrongs. But what a pleasure it was to talk shop with a fellow connoisseur of violence.

Hound gave his wheezing Tumbleside laugh. "Keep your hand in, Ebrin, and Lowtown boys'll be no match for you."

"What about Thrani?" the Vinculine asked suddenly.

"Not my turf, the Quarter. I hear they're soft, though."

The silence lengthened. Hound knew when to cut the banter with the Vinculine. Their talk had left him restless, though. He pulled out pouch and pipe, filled the pipe with yellow-gray strands of snakeweed, and prepared to strike a spark.

"Don't."

Pale gaze met dark, questioning.

"No time for that. We're going out." Ebrin stood. His good humor had returned. "Ever had your fortune told?"

Sandhound grimaced. "I don't let anybody pull that shit on me."

"Perhaps Santha Seona will change your mind—set some bones to roasting and tell you the names of the last five men you killed."

"If the Santha knows *that*, one Thrani is dog's meat."

The Vinculine laughed. "Easy, Hound. Let the creature live awhile. I may have a use for it."

No guards accompanied them to the Thrani Quarter. Hooded and cloaked, the two men moved with the gait—half swagger, half stealth—typical of Low Xalycis by night. They were enjoying themselves, almost hoping some fool would challenge them in one of the unlit alleys.

When they came to Bonereaders Court, the Vinculine threw back his hood and resumed his air of authority. His request that the Santha see him had the ring of an order.

"Another visitor—" the doorman began.

"We'll wait. Within reason." The Vinculine tossed him a coin, then brushed past into the oracle's house.

Servants brought them honey cakes and thick, spiced moka. Two children, roused from sleep, were ushered in to sing for the guests. Their high, pure voices joined flawlessly, until Sandhound startled them with a howl and they broke off, staring. The paint around their eyes gave them the look of small owls.

"Will you come please, sers?" Shrouded in rustling fabric, their new guide glided before them along dim corridors to Santha Seona's audience chamber.

The scent of acrid smoke lingered in the room, where the fire pit gaped uncovered. Tall candles burned on either side of the Santha's curtained throne. The Vinculine crossed to the throne and bowed with profound respect. "Most reverend Santha."

" *'Ei Vincul Chroze.*" The words resounded in Seona's deepest tone, like the plucking of long harpstrings. The Bound King: A title so old it was the same in Thrani and Xalycan.

"*Santha Maheira,*" Ebrin declared in turn. Twice-Born Wisdom. Thus did the Thrani address that rare and marvelous abomination, a hermaphrodite with the power to read the bones. "I have come to you for counsel." A brief hesitation, and then he continued resolutely. "In their hunger for magic, my people—the good citizens of Low Xalycis—are beggaring themselves over relicts true and false. No edict from the Council can stop them. I could arrest every maker, every shopkeeper who's gone grubbing for treasure in the Tumbles, and ten more would spring up in his place. They will not believe that the old magic is dead."

"Is it dead?" Contralto, the voice of a beautiful woman. The concealing curtain stirred with some movement behind it.

"So the Academy insists." The Vinculine spoke blandly, shrugging as though to apologize for the scholars' inadequacy.

Sandhound watched this performance, instinct keeping him silent though he had no idea what Ebrin was after.

"Tell me, Santha," the Vinculine demanded, "is this a passing madness? Or has the Artifact brought a plague beyond any man's controlling?"

"This is what you would have me ask the bones?"

"It is."

An ambiguous sound that might be a sigh. "The old, the dark, the wise ones. To burn such a treasure . . . ah, *Vincul*, you ask much. Much."

Ebrin unlaced his tunic and drew out a roll of cloth bound with cord. He opened it to disclose something that gleamed in the candlelight. Sandhound crept a little closer. Double-orrins, bright gold, each half the size of a man's palm—a fortune. Murder bait anywhere in Lowtown. A muscle twitched in Sandhound's face.

"Will this suffice?"

Even the Santha seemed overwhelmed. The changeable voice came out flatly, after a moment's silence. "Yes. Yes it will." And the curtain around the throne hissed back, to disclose a massive form swathed in deep indigo, like part of the night set in motion, rising and flowing with slow grace past the Vinculine and his proferred treasure, to come to rest by the fire pit.

A signal must have been given, for the door at the back of the chamber opened and a manservant glided in. They all moved like ghosts, these Thrani.

Santha Seona issued a rapid burst of orders that sent the servant straight out again, to return bearing a black enameled box with as much care as though it held his living soul. Inside, resting on velvet, was the whole of a skeletal hand, deeply discolored by centuries in vault or tomb. Grotesquely, rings hung loose upon each finger, winking with gems.

When the fire had been stirred to life again, and laced with dark salts that burned violet under a pall of smoke, the servant used two slender wood rods to lift the hand, slowly so the rings slid, rattling, but did not fall. When it touched the fire, the bones emitted a loud crack. Flame surged up.

The sound of the door closing behind the departing servant roused Sandhound from rapt contemplation of the fire pit, ablaze like a burning city. He could almost see smoldering roofs, toppling walls, through the smoke, the drifting sparks. But Hound knew the ways of black *khur*. He made his breathing shallow, resisted the urge to fly with the sparks or sink into the mysteries of bone. How was Ebrin taking it? He turned to look. Sweet hell! Grinning like a skull, mantled in blood, demonic. . . . When Hound blinked, the nightmare image vanished. The Vinculine sat safely back from the pit, eyes intelligent and alert above the corner of cloak he held to his face, watching the Santha's deepening trance.

Then Seona spoke.

"It is dry tinder in a man, waiting. Waiting to reach with hands of flame and pull down heaven. Universal madness. The Mad King. Like master, like man." The veiled figure rocked on its haunches, leaning into the smoke, drawing back. A new voice was emerging, thin, ironic, lacking the eerie music of the double sex. "So little change!" it burst out in exasperation. There should have been some angry gesture to accompany the words, but the oracle's shrouded bulk merely swayed, forward, back, like a signpost swinging idly in the wind. "Well, then. Ask me your questions. Who are you?"

Ebrin let the cloak drop from his face and grinned. "Lord of Misrule."

Flame reached deeper into the bone—again it cracked. Two of the fingers collapsed, and the skeletal hand shifted on its bed of ash.

Sandhound could not help himself. "Hurry it up," he muttered. "No time for your damn jokes."

The Vinculine recognized the urgency as well. It was time for the real question, the thing he had come for. The words clung in his throat, then tumbled out: "The Artifact, Seona, can Seona reach the mind within the Artifact, past all its wards?"

A muted crackling, as coals settled in the seamed bones. The sparks hissed on a rising current of air, winking out suddenly. Santha Seona's movements had slowed. Ebrin was about to speak again, with greater force, when the voice of the bones finally replied. "The oracle can pass within and speak for what is there."

"In the Artifact?"

"Yesss." The word sank into the sounds of the dying fire.

Sandhound glanced at Ebrin, who was frowning, lost in thought, then deliberately spat into the fire pit. "Show's over. What about the gold?"

The double-orrins still lay untouched where the Vinculine had set them down.

"Leave it." Ebrin rose. "Funds for the revolution."

"What?"

"Surely they won't stand still after I have the Santha arrested." Smiling, he rang the bell to summon the servants. "Not a word, Hound."

Hound nodded, watching until the Vinculine's gaze grew vague with dreams again. Then his hand darted into the fire pit, emerging with ash-covered trophies. Let the Thrani have their orrins; he would play at dice with their ancestor's fingerbone, and sport a flash pair of old rings. Why not? This was the high life now!

IX

Prodigal Sons

The throngs still came, with good reason. The newest finery, freshest gossip, latest opinions, were always to be found at the Blue Lion. If it was just a little daring to frequent such a place, so much the better. Perhaps the Vinculine might appear tonight. (Who would he find to replace the Raven? Wags said he had arrested Santha Seona not for policy, but pleasure.) The worthies of Wallwalk chattered, glittered, formed and re-formed in shifting constellations, an iridescent froth, volatile yet conscribed as the permutations of a relict.

"Innmaster Rodion, such marvelous party favors—"

"Innmaster, I don't believe you've met my wife—"

"My dear fellow, would you care to discuss a matter of business?"

"You're quiet tonight, Innmaster. Has the Vinculine confiscated your tongue? Ha ha ha!"

Their laughter, their whispers, crowded around him until Rodion could scarcely breathe. And still he smiled, summoning up new banter, flourishing his bright sleeves, chiefest ornament of his own inn.

He could gladly have murdered them all.

But desperation drove Gherifan Arnix no farther than an unfashionable side street at an unfashionably early hour. Plain-clad, hair neatly bound back, he looked close kin to the Leandric Gath who had once paid a call upon the Widow Murn. He stood soberly at a vine-hung gate in the cliff's shadow. Anyone might have thought he had been sent, like Gath, to collect a debt. Gherifan waited while a servant delivered his message—a single line of verse on a folded page with a light scent of sandalwood.

When he heard her step, he looked up, blandly polite.

Jesimis-nenna surveyed him through the opened gate. "Why, butter wouldn't melt in its anonymous little mouth."

His gaze took on an almost lunatic sincerity. "Sera, I've come about the drains."

She choked back a caw of laughter and pulled him in from the lane.

Gravel path, parched courtyard, miniature flight of steps, he followed her to the sudden luxury of a terrace canopied with silk and scattered with bright cushions.

"Your father's old steward treats you well."

"Better than I deserve?" She waved him to a seat and settled herself some distance away. For a woman in seclusion, she seemed extraordinarily vivid. The rich violet of her gown intensified as she took an orange from a dish beside her and began to tease away the skin in bright spirals.

Half-hypnotized, he watched her and did not reply.

"Such gallantry, ser," she mocked. "Such streams of eloquence as I haven't heard for many a day."

"Rodion is talked out, so you're left with plain Gherifan," he said. "Will he do?"

"Yes." The orange lay bare in her hand, and she smiled at him.

Gherifan could not muster an answering smile. "Ebrin wants to wield the Artifact," he began abruptly. "His guards have arrested Santha Seona on some trumped-up charge, but there's only one reason he'd have need of a bonereader."

"He's taken the Santha?" Jesimis sat very still. "I'd almost forgotten. . . . Once, when we were first together, we made the rounds of the fortune tellers. One look at us, and they'd know what to say, but they peered into their crystals, scanned entrails or meditated over basins of holy water before they came out with it. Never such a love as ours—et cetera. Only Seona spoke differently, said I must save myself or be consumed in the fire. I thought it was a strange old prude's moralizing and laughed it off. Hendor must have known even then it was the truth."

"Now the city's in love with him."

"My dear—" She rested a palm on his shoulder. The scent of oranges lingered on her skin. "You've helped one foolish woman escape the consequences of her folly. It's quite another thing to save the world."

He stared straight into her eyes. "Tell me everything you know about Ebrin. What makes him laugh, how he deals with a problem, what he reads, what music moves him—"

"How he performs in bed?" Jesimis had drawn away. The air between them seemed to spark with her anger. "That will speed you in your quest. Invaluable, to discover where Xalycis should place her legs when he has her down."

"You were well suited," he said—words like a slap in the face. "Get yourself a steady source of news, and you should enjoy the next few years, watching everyone behave at his worst. A pageant for the cynic."

"What an end to your schoolboy romance," she answered with a matching brutality. "That melancholy Sera Vuorn wasn't such a nice woman after all, and your beloved city turns out to be a slut with an appetite for the lash.''

"So my father and Murn begged to be slaughtered? Is that it? They loved the sight of their own blood.''

Her fury vanished as swiftly as it had come. "Gherifan, forgive me. I should have remembered—I never think before I speak."

Awkwardly, he waved off the apology. "Will you help me?" he asked with a new diffidence.

"Any way I can."

"So you see what Ebrin's up to?" Gherifan leaned back in the chair, his face receding into shadows. The candle on the innmaster's desk concentrated its fire in the glass lion.

"Why didn't you bring me into this before?" Railu demanded.

"Without proof—no. I've been crazy enough these past months without bringing you in."

"I'd've slit the bastard's throat for you."

Gherifan's abrupt movement set the candle flame leaping. "And make him a martyr, while you went to the gallows? Dancer, I want him to *fall*, and know he's falling, with the whole city watching."

In the half-light, Knifedancer's features had a feral sharpness. "All right. I'm with you."

"Can you bring in some men you trust, from the Guild?"

"Better than that. You say the Vinculine's after magic? What if we had magic of our own?"

Gherifan frowned. "Your Shandar thing? I thought—"

"Nothing to do with it. Except Dalu's in on this too." Railu was grinning. "You'd be surprised what's going on up at Vuorn House."

"Vuorn." The word touched a nerve.

"Scared of your kin next door?" A teasing glint in the

green eyes. "Now if you lived in Lowtown, cheek by jowl, Arnix brats on Vuorn's landings, Vuorn's essences reeking in the Arnix halls. . . . I can almost see it."

"So can I, hoof-head. Get on with it."

For the first time, Railu noticed how tired his friend looked, behind the brash beard and the finery. "All right," he said simply. "That woman who made the prophecy, in a fit at your old man's table? She's there. She and Vuorn and Dalu and that maker who did my pigment, they're all working on some crazy thing with perfume and relicts. Don't ask me to explain it."

Innmaster Rodion, widely credited with omniscience, had known nothing of this strange gathering of forces. "You trust them, do you?"

"Dalu Chemic has never stepped off the True Road in his life."

"The others, I meant," Gherifan interposed, with a shrug of apology.

"Trust. . . ." Leaning back in his chair, Railu scrutinized the shadowed ceiling. "Well," he continued after a pause, "they trust *me*, you see. And they'd lose more by it, if I turned traitor." Another pause. "Things the Vinculine wants, they *don't*."

"Then I'm their man," Gherifan said softly.

The dancer chuckled. "Wrapped in ribbons like a nameday gift, and rolled through the door. They'll love you, Gherro."

Magic against magic, thought Gherifan Arnix. And despite himself, he felt a tremor of raw fear.

In his one sober suit of clothes, the master of the Blue Lion came to Vuorn House. A gust of wind through its banner bells made him start nervously. Railu tightened his grip on Gherifan's arm. "Damnit, Gherro, calm down."

"How can I be calm in brown linen, without a hundred people jostling around me?" Gherifan attempted a grin. "Just lead me to my fate, Dancer."

Even in a great house as eccentric as Vuorn's, the elegant apparatus of a well-trained staff brought a visitor from the door to his destination with the hushed grace of a solemn rite. A younger Gherifan used to run through his father's house, yelling. The grown man walked, thinking of Jesimis pacing these halls.

The woman at Vuorn's side was another creature altogether. How could Dancer have said he once fancied her, before Clerk Stilpin moved in? Stilpin was welcome to his little percept, with her narrow shoulders and devouring eyes. Lifelong, she'd keep the look of a precocious child.

Gherifan bowed. "Vuorn. Sera Shar." And on through the others in the room, Stilpin, Dalu, Lodvin.

With a fine disregard for Wallwalk manners, Railu had already left him and taken a seat beside Lodvin. Now Dalu Chemic rose with a grunt of impatience. "My grand-nephew says you have days' worth to tell us, Gherifan Arnix, and a few hours to do it in. Best get on with it. Eh, Vuorn?"

The master of Vuorn House led Gherifan to a chair a little apart from the others. Center stage. Gherifan cleared his throat. "I've been trying to learn something about my father's murder. So . . . this present guise." He fingered his gingery beard. "I thought at first it must be Low City work. The manner of the theft, the waste and . . . the brutality. So I went where I could listen to Lowtown rumor, study the villains at close hand. Scoring the Artifact, that's a *tremendous* coup. It ought to leave tracks everywhere. Maybe the killer's own corpse as well, in time. Even a bold thief can be bested, especially when the stakes are high. I was a fool, of course, to think I could stir up the muck— even Jabel Fivesides's fancier sort of muck—and see my way clear. But I had fool's luck, stumbling over part of the truth before I'd been at it long enough to know better. I met the Widow Murn.''

The tale unfolded before a silent audience. As Gherifan spoke, he found himself falling back into some of Rodion's mannerisms. He needed the innmaster's bravado. Without it, he would be obvious as flawed glass in strong sunlight, each fleck and blur of cowardice, shoddy reasoning, self-love, and misplaced lust magnified intolerably. Yet he felt the mask wearing dangerously thin under the percept's scrutiny—and Vuorn's, the look of a man with a half-healed wound.

Speaking of the city's danger, Gherifan faltered. He could not rid himself of Jesimis's taunting image of the city as a slut eager for her own pain at a master's hands. What magic could counter the Vinculine's glamor?

"It's just as you said, 'Bet," Stilpin burst out. "Power calling to power. Do you think Ebrin has a chance of getting through the Artifact's wards with Seona's help?"

Wards. Gherifan was instantly alert, his previous unease forgotten.

The percept held her hand to her throat. "That's who I saw. It frightened me so, I had to pull back, but I should have recognized . . . Stilpin, it will mean Seona's death. That blue fleck, it's only the beginning of a terrible process. The Artifact still has all of its defenses."

"Then Seona can't get through?" Gherifan returned to Stilpin's question with a dawning hope.

"If the bonereader fails, Ebrin will seek elsewhere." Vuorn's gaze moved from Moabet to Lodvin, then turned toward Dalu for confirmation. "Our experiments could be used to his advantage."

Stilpin stifled an oath.

Railu was frowning. "Sounds like you're in worse trouble than Gherro here."

"No." The percept spoke decisively. "Gherifan faces the most danger of any of us."

"What do you mean?" He wondered if she could have misread him as a hothead avenger after all.

There was no condescension or pity in her eyes. "Gherifan, tell us how Hendor Ebrin would describe his plans for the future."

He shivered at the thought. Aside from some minor mimicry, his characters had always been invented. To crawl beneath the skin of such a man . . . ! Yet even as he shrank from it, Gherifan found himself remembering tones of voice, gestures, phrases that Jesimis had passed along to him, and he drew them on like a familiar suit of clothes.

"In this company, I know better than to speak my mind," Hendor Ebrin said with a self-deprecating smile.

Even Moabet looked startled at the transformation. Railu clutched at an amulet around his neck, and Dalu muttered a swift prayer. Silent Lodvin had an odd look, something like approval.

Gherifan banished the specter with haste, saying in his own voice, "It's not as though I can read his thoughts. Anyone could tell you what he'd say."

"Not as you just did," Moabet countered. "It's a relict talent—like my gift, or curse. Something the mages used to the full, while we stumble along in the dark."

"What would a mage want with an actor?" He was skeptical.

The percept seemed to draw her reply from a distance, as though she had not known it till she spoke. "A mutable mind, not bound to one form of being. A center easily discarded. An intensity that might harden into self-regard given enough time, but catch it early and you have a source of power ready to your hand. It could last for centuries before it went quite mad. And then—get another."

"Arkhenazuril." Stilpin was the first to understand. To Gherifan, he said, "That's the Artifact. A mad thing. Moabet was able to touch its mind."

Gherifan shuddered. "If I get near it, this thing will . . . devour me? Is that what you're saying?"

"If the Vinculine knew you for what you are, he might find a way to make that happen." Moabet's hands clenched, and her voice was tight. "Revitalized, the Artifact might respond to him at last."

"Damnit!" Gherifan cried. "Is all your magic doomed to serve *him*? I don't see what use in hell it can have for me." He was on his feet. "There's no point in my taking up more of your time."

"Gherifan." The percept held him with her gaze. "Ebrin can be stopped. Arkhenazuril is the key. We'll find a way to turn it."

"Can't we just steal the thing ourselves and get rid of it?" asked Railu. "That's what Gherro had in mind all along, and it sounds like a good plan. After all, Ebrin grabbed it—it didn't do anything to him."

"It wasn't fully awake then."

"So why doesn't it destroy him now?"

She shook her head. "He's keeping his distance, I suspect."

A ghost of an idea entered Gherifan's mind. He pursued it—and was seized by hands of ice. In his fear, he might have blurted it out, to be reassured of its impossibility, but Lodvin forestalled him by joining the conversation at last.

"We've been talking about magic." Lodvin looked around him as though to confirm this fact. "Maybe it does all follow the mages' pattern if we think in their terms. Stealing an object or a soul, countering power with a bigger power . . . that's their way, and the Vinculine's." Another pause. They indicated their agreement, unwilling to interrupt this speech. "The thing is, you don't have to do that. Even the highest talent, the acting—well, Mother still says Father could have won away her whole audience with his tricks, if he'd wanted to."

Railu leaned toward Gherifan and muttered, "His mother's Margola, father was a stage chemic named Chityr."

Gherifan's eyes widened.

With an absent nod, Lodvin went on. "He could do wonderful things. More than he ever showed on stage, where the players only needed a little smoke, some colored lights, to make you see almost anything or anybody. At home, in his workshop, Father liked to do what he called his 'play magic.' Sometimes he'd show me. Locks would break open at a few passes of his hand. There was a flock of metal birds—oh, they were beautiful when they sang! But he specially liked turning things invisible. Not really, you understand, but with black cloths and special boxes, masks and cloaks. We'd sometimes hide from Mother," he grinned. "She hated that." The grin faded. "When he died, she wouldn't let anyone touch his workshop. It's all still there. The notebooks, the chemic's gear. What I wish"—he turned to Vuorn with a sudden fervor—"is that he could have met you. He didn't know much perfume lore, or he might have used essences in his disguises."

Stilpin and Moabet exchanged glances.

Vuorn was stroking his beard. "Perfume masks. I wanted to try them when I was a lad, but my master would have none of it. 'Violating every canon of our high art . . .' He made it sound like a dreadful crime. Obedient lad that I was, I forgot all about the matter. I suspect your father would have pursued it."

Gherifan's mind was a jumble of wild notions, half-formed

as that terrifying idea from which he still shied. Better, far better, to ask Lodvin, "Could your father's illusions fool the Artifact—or lull it in some way?"

"I don't know. There's a lot he didn't tell me. And Mother—well, I don't go home very often. I suppose she doesn't trust me to handle what he left behind."

Railu raised his eyes to the heavens. Then he was on his feet. "Your mother. Margola . . . she needs a talking to." He paced the room, a tawny panther. "Just because she's the greatest player the city's ever known, just because she was beautiful and had all the men hot for her"—he cast a wicked glance at Dalu—"that doesn't mean she can lord it over the world. Loddy has rights! Time he took what's his." Railu favored them with his most seductive smile. "Or maybe we just have to persuade her."

As a babble of talk broke out, Gherifan remained quiet. Lost in his thoughts, he had become supremely unobtrusive. He pondered invisibility, masks, illusions. No need for him to avail himself of Chityr's bag of tricks. Rodion of Rhune, master of the Blue Lion, could vanish like a burst bubble at any moment. He imagined himself floating free, bodiless, solitary . . . futile. The brief exhilaration left him. Exit Gath, exit Rodion, another player must take the stage. When he closed his eyes he could see a figure bold as the hero of a melodrama, clear as his own reflection: Gherifan Arnix's most challenging role. He gave a wry smile. They would say he had been born to the part.

When the innmaster vanished, High Xalycis buzzed with rumors. He had died in a midnight duel, been found with his hand in the till and sent packing (or to a quiet grave), the Vinculine had seized him as a foreign spy, an amorous matron pursued him till he fled. He was an imposter from

Lowtown—liar, murderer, thief. He was a true prince, gone back west to come into his kingdom. One of the city's obscurer sects even claimed that Rodion had been a disguised god, surveying the wicked at close hand. (Woe to the unbeliever, in these coming times!)

A week after Rodion's disappearance, Gherifan Arnix returned to his ancestral home, crop-haired, clean-shaven, and vague about his whereabouts in the past months.

"Heard you were looking for me," he said.

Berec scanned his brother's face for signs of insolence, found them, drummed his fingers on the huge teak desk that had been Aubric's, and sighed. Would Gherifan *never* grow up? "Brother," he began.

"Yes, Brother?"

"You recall the provisions of Father's will? The estate to pass down undivided, with assurance that you would always be provided for."

Gherifan said nothing, but smiled slightly.

"Well, he also left further bequests to my discretion. After his passing, I had an extensive inventory conducted, and determined that some of his collections could be sold without affecting the overall value of the estate. Therefore," he cleared his throat. "If you wish it"—Berec avoided his brother's eyes—"the contents of the Rose Room are yours."

Gherifan let out a whoop. "The pornography! Gods, I'd almost forgotten that time we bribed our way in and got an eyeful. Decided to mend your ways, have you?"

Berec winced, at the vulgar Lowtown whine as much as the mockery. The Rose Room was all too appropriate a bequest. "Among Father's collections, this one seemed . . . dispensable," he replied, keeping his voice even. "Ah yes," he added, opening a small, plain box. "The key."

Gherifan grinned. "To the Gates of Paradise."

"Or the other place," Berec muttered, handing over the key as though it might burn him.

Gherifan trailed a reply over his shoulder, as he predictably left without taking formal leave. It sounded like, "So I come into my kingdom. . . ." Berec shook his head. He must have misheard. Or else Gherifan was truly mad.

Cloud House stood on a quiet street near the crest of a steep slope, unlikely as a phoenix in a flock of pigeons. It stretched wings of white ribbed stone skyward, to dazzle and dissolve in light. On either side, the stolid dwellings of ordinary mortals had an air of pinch-faced disapproval.

Railu Knifedancer whistled. "Your dad conjure that up in a night?"

"He designed it, but it took years to build. He wouldn't let Mother see it until it was finished." Lodvin squinted against the brightness. "When I was little, she told me the sprites made it for us. Her callers thought it was only her due—a white tower for the Goddess. She still has a book with all their poems."

"Anyone call on her now?"

Lodvin shook his head. "Not many. She thinks they're too old, the ones left from those days."

"Then I'll have a clear field, won't I?"

The door servant was no creaking ancient, but a Thrani boy with impudent eyes. Too young to know Lodvin by sight, he stared both men up and down. Margola had trained him out of Thrani silence, and he asked their business pertly. When he returned with her reply, he waited, smiling, until Lodvin slipped him a coin, then showed them into the house.

The salon had an outworn air. The spare, elegant furnishings had grown brittle with the years, and a keen eye might spot worn places in the gauze curtains billowing where unseen fans raised the semblance of a summer breeze. But the wine was excellent, and the waiting beguiled by a flute somewhere just out of sight, weaving intricate melodies.

The flute stopped in mid-note as Margola swept into the room. Railu had expected gaudy artifice or lushness gone to seed, but not this: a tall, slim woman with perfect bones and a presence like a storm, crackling, a little dangerous. She wore a deep blue gown and headcloth and a single ornament, a shoulder pin in the shape of a mask, silver and serene. Only by an act of will could one penetrate to the deep lines at mouth and brow, the gauntness of age. And seeing them could not dispel the sense that Margola had preserved the miracle of her beauty unchanged, eternal.

"Mother," Lodvin said. "This is my friend, Railu Knife-dancer. He works at the Blue Lion."

"Star of the show, I'm told." She favored the dancer with an appraising glance. "I keep up with the outer world, you see." Margola's voice was low and melodious, transforming commonplace to poetry. "Come, here beside me." She sat erect in a tall, slim chair, gesturing to a stack of cushions nearby.

Was this where her worshipers had once gathered around her, a puddle of adoring young men? Railu sank gracefully onto the cushions and looked up, into her dark eyes.

"What brings you here?" she asked. "My son seems quite a stranger now."

Already cowed, Lodvin muttered something that could have been apology or feeble defiance. Margola paid him no attention.

"Without the pigment he cooked up, I'd be dancing naked." Railu gave her a lazy smile, which faded as his gaze grew more intense. "Then he told me about you. I was wild to rush right up, of course."

"He discouraged you?" Margola asked, a certain menace in her tone.

"Well, you see, my grand-uncle is a chemic, and Loddy thought it might seem I was prying into your husband's things if I came here. But I told him, I'm no spy. It's Margola I want to see, and besides, Dalu Chemic is the match of anyone living or dead, so why should I pry into a dusty workshop?" He leaned a little farther back, his head not far from Margola's knee. "Begging your pardon, sera."

"How absurd," she replied with a laugh once legendary on the stage. "How could Loddy think I would begrudge his friends? You must bear with me, though, my dear Knife-dancer, for I intend to prove you wrong."

"Wrong?" he echoed dutifully.

"About my late husband. He was no ordinary chemic, you see—begging your pardon, ser," a mocking glance. "Chityr worked miracles not even the mages could have equaled. Have you ever seen the like of Cloud House?"

"Never! Magnificent as its mistress."

"Flatterer." Margola ruffled his hair with one long-fingered hand, as though he were a mischievous, favored dog. "My late husband designed this house."

"Really? How amazing! I had no idea."

Lodvin cast a reproachful look at Railu for this dissembling, but remained silent.

"I shall show you every room—including the workshops—a grand tour. Call it a penance for your ignorance." Her indulgent expression took any sting from the words.

"Teach me, then. I'll go back and tell Grand-uncle he's a dabbler."

"Brave lad." She rose. In one lithe motion, he was standing beside her. Margola turned toward the door, then added over her shoulder, "Oh, Loddy. You can come too. We might need a chaperon."

As Railu gallantly took her arm, he felt a little giddy with success. The percept's plan had worked so well, Moabet might have scripted the whole conversation. A turn on the stage with Margola! Railu grinned to himself. Who said Gherifan Arnix was the only player with a gift? Gherro should be here to see him now. He'd be wild with envy.

X

The Honor of the House

Berec i-Arnix began to curse the day he had wished for his brother's safe return. Nothing but trouble seemed to have come from it. Back in the comforts of Arnix House, Gherifan was a maddening, unpredictable presence who might plummet from hilarity to sullen brooding between two breaths. Worse, he seemed to have a following among the servants. A few of them refused outright to report on his behavior—even claimed to find it natural, "for a young man with his father killed in such a fashion."

Weakness! That's what it amounted to, thought Berec. Father had let the boy run wild. It was time Gherifan learned some social graces.

"I've arranged a modest dinner party in honor of your return," Berec informed Gherifan one morning. "Your attendance is requested."

"Shall I appear as the third course, stewed to a turn?" Gherifan asked.

Berec did not dignify the question with a reply.

Gherifan ironically crossed arms upon chest. "I surrender, Brother! But tell me, who are you subjecting to my presence?"

"Artem and Cire from Prasc House, Bel from Danion, Dagnis Nur . . ."

Brows rising, Gherifan said, "Such trust. Loosing the serpent among the dull dogs. Though I suppose they're sworn to silence if I misbehave."

"I won't stake the reputation of this house on your behavior," Berec acknowledged stiffly.

Gherifan struck a new pose. "I shall be tedious as mud, discreet as a locked tomb."

Much to Berec's surprise, Gherifan *did* comport himself well throughout the evening. There was something almost uncanny about his good manners. The way he listened to Artemon Prasc describe his plans for a new garden pool edged with ancestral portraits in mosaic—solemnly attentive. His delicacy with the ladies, each compliment to young Cirissa Prasc followed after some moments by an equal flourish directed at the Widow Dagnis. Indeed, Berec committed to memory some of Gherifan's most apt remarks, for use in further conversations with the attractive widow. Such fine sentiments, they could have been Berec's own words.

Indeed, they might have been, for Gherifan had mastered his brother's mannerisms to perfection. Only Cirissa got the joke—she stifled her giggles and joined Gherifan in a conspiracy of two, doing her best to imitate her own sententious brother. Gherifan had to give her a warning look, lest the foolery go too far; he had a purpose tonight, and it was vital that Berec not know he was being mocked.

When the guests had departed, Berec conscientiously rewarded Gherifan's good behavior with a civil bow and a few words of praise.

Gherifan had the grace to look embarrassed. "Here, in this room where Father held so many famous dinners, I realized what it meant to be an Arnix. We have to keep the tradition alive—not just for our friends, but for the great men who could find a little peace, good fellowship, over Arnix wine. Where can those councilors go now, except some foul place like the Blue Lion? We're letting them down if we keep to ourselves. More than that, we're betraying Father's memory. It came to me in a flash, Berec. It's we who must bear his burden now."

Berec was much moved by this speech. Perhaps he had misjudged his young brother. A sensitive lad, given to unfortunate moods, yet he had a good heart. "I'm a bit of a recluse, I suppose," he acknowledged. "Dagnis seems happy enough in my company—still, she might like to preside over a really splendid table like Father's. A famous hostess."

"And a famous host," Gherifan added. "No need to underrate yourself. They were hanging on your every word tonight."

A complacent smile dawned on Berec's face. He had suffered from his father's scorn, the great men's snubs. Could he flourish at last, out of Aubric i-Arnix's huge shadow? "Whom should we invite?" he asked, forgetting his vow never to request Gherifan's opinion on any matter of importance.

Gherifan's eyes flashed. "Why not go for the top? The Vinculine."

Father's special crony. The very thought of him made Berec nervous, but this was not a time for timidity. They must act boldly and reclaim the glory of a great house. "The Vinculine it is!" he cried.

Fortunately, he did not see the fleeting look of pity his brother gave him. Berec was pouring the last of the wine into two glasses, so he might propose a toast: "To Arnix!"

Gherifan echoed him, down to his very gesture. "To Arnix!"

Berec was too buoyed by his success to notice that the party for the Vinculine began with certain ominous signs. The Councilor, for instance: he had been at that fated dinner where the percept had made her prophecy of doom. And he came alone this time. If Berec had spent any time at the Blue Lion, he would have known the whole tale behind the desertion of the Councilor's wife, dismayed when her husband's lifelong dullness gave way to increasingly immoderate new appetites. A party could not remain entirely sober in the presence of Councilman Trinth. As for Gherifan, somehow it did not come to Berec's attention that his brother wore an ominously somber shade of gray and contributed only grudging monosyllables to the conversation while the party waited for its guest of honor. The Vinculine's lateness made Berec somewhat nervous, of course, but he assured himself that the great man had been delayed by some crisis of state.

Indeed, the Vinculine bustled in at last with an air of important business about him, and made graceful apology for his tardiness. So they were five at table ("just an informal little gathering of friends," as Berec had put it in the personal note he appended to each invitation): Berec proudly at the head, with Hendor Ebrin to his right, Dagnis Nur to his left, and the Councilman and Gherifan almost lost behind the profusion of cutlery, roast fowl, pastries, and decanters that made up the first course.

An odd number, an unlikely group, just what Aubric i-Arnix had reveled in. Yet, as his first flush of accomplishment faded, Berec became obscurely uncomfortable. By the time of the second course, the talk had grown quite free. Should he signal to the servants that they were too prompt in refilling half-empty wineglasses? No, that would show him for a prude. And he should take pride in the way the Vinculine flirted with Dagnis; no matter if her answering smile seemed a trifle warm. At least Gherifan was subdued in the presence of his betters.

Berec had no clear-eyed percept at his side to present the party in its true light, as a program for disaster. Dagnis Nur, amiable, not very witty, was charming Berec and boring the Vinculine out of his own expansive mood in equal measure. Councilman Trinth sat almost hypnotized by Ebrin despite his past humiliation at the Vinculine's hands. As for Hendor Ebrin, an alert observer would have seen in him a quality of casual danger, a beast half sleeping, half sated, but liable to rouse at the scent of new prey. And Gherifan Arnix? With every glass of wine he grew more sullen. He had begun to flinch from the Vinculine's passing gaze, with the injured look of too-sensitive adolescence, as though he'd shed five years in returning to Arnix House. Before long, Ebrin would take note of him and find a fitting source of amusement at last.

But Ebrin's boredom was to find a quicker remedy. Sipping sweet, chilled wine, Dagnis Nur gave a little shiver. "It's almost like drinking blood, isn't it? So very *red*."

Berec was laboriously composing a tribute to the nectar that no doubt ran in the lady's veins (hoping this fancy would not be deemed indelicate) when Gherifan shattered his empty glass against the wall behind him and drew his thumb across one jagged edge. "Just the thing for our friend the Vinculine. He has already supped on Arnix blood. Would you care for a second helping, Ebrin?"

The Vinculine had a complex expression, at once puzzled, solicitous, and—if one judged only by the quirk of the lips —almost pleased to be the object of attack.

Berec i-Arnix stared, openmouthed and speechless.

Remarkably, Dagnis kept her head, wrapping a napkin around Gherifan's bleeding hand, murmuring, "Foolish boy.

Now why did you do that?" as Gherifan continued to stare at Ebrin.

Who finally spoke: "These sanguinary metaphors, Gherifan, I don't quite see their purpose. Am I to understand I leeched away your father's fortune?" He glanced around the elegant room.

That drew an injudicious laugh from Councilman Trinth. Berec, recovering from his first shock, was beginning to sputter.

With one word, Gherifan produced complete silence and drew every gaze to him. "Murder." An impressive utterance, from a pale young man with burning eyes.

The Vinculine leaned back in his chair, apparently quite at ease. "A serious charge. Based on—what? A rumor? A dream?" He gave a rueful smile, wide mouth comically crimped. "Or a redirected sense of guilt?" The smile faded. "You know, there was some talk of questioning you after the killing. Nothing came of it, of course, and the Helm never pursued the matter. Your long . . . absence was noted, however."

That brought Berec half out of his chair. "Are you suggesting—?"

Gherifan ignored his brother. Still he fixed his full attention on Hendor Ebrin. "You were the last to see him. You dined together. What more natural than for him to show you his treasure vault, and his latest prize? You couldn't bear for another man to possess it, could you?"

"My dear boy, you have it backward. Your father could never have bought the Artifact if he hadn't a friend in high places to ease the way. Some in the Council quite resented it going to a private buyer instead of staying in City hands."

Gherifan's voice rose, with a new edge of desperation. "You killed him for the thrill of it, then, and took the Artifact as a kind of trophy!"

"Thrills are best left to the young," Ebrin declared. His eyes were grave. "You blame me for failing to catch the murderer, don't you? The death of my old friend, so soon after I had spent that pleasant evening with him here, a loss so shattering . . . and the mighty Vinculine is helpless. Justice has not been served. Gherifan—" he reached out his hand. "It's true that I've failed you. Forgive me?"

Berec made to speak, but the Vinculine silenced him with a look. Ebrin's outstretched arm held rock-steady, the hand open, beseeching, manifestly honest. "Help me, Gherifan. Perhaps together we can do what I alone could not."

Gherifan's sternness dissolved in uncertainty. Hesitantly, like a shy child endeavoring to play the man, he took the offered hand.

They exchanged a solid grip. As the contact broke, the Vinculine said, "Now tell us, why did you bring this up tonight, at your brother's table? Did you think my fellow guests would accept your theories?"

A mute nod.

"Well, perhaps they *can* help us in other ways. Councilman Trinth." (The man jerked to attention, the picture of guilt.) "Did anything strike you as unusual about Aubric i-Arnix when you last saw him?"

"He was all right. It was that crazy outlander girl ruined the evening with her talk of death and doom." Trinth's eyes widened. "Maybe she was in with the killer, and that's how she knew."

Dagnis choked back an exclamation of horror. "Foreigners did it!"

Gherifan shook his head. "I thought of that, but if the Artifact had fallen into their hands, wouldn't we know by now? The Thrani seem helpless with their Santha gone, and the Shandar are busy fawning over their capering dancer. It's as though the Artifact had vanished from the world." He struck the table with his good hand, and shouted, "Somebody's making fools of us!"

Berec had recovered enough from his shock to say at last, "Esteemed Ser Vinculine, I cannot apologize too deeply for my brother's ill-considered outburst. He has been under a great deal of strain, and I should have realized—"

Ebrin waved him off. "Please, my dear i-Arnix, you have nothing to be ashamed of. I wish I saw more of Gherifan's zealousness among my own assistants, let alone the men of the Helm. Xalycis is too old a city, too wary of youth and passion. You have no idea how refreshing it is to encounter them in full flower."

Gherifan looked a little sullen at this, or perhaps he was still sulking over Berec's remarks.

The Vinculine raised his glass with a flourish. "Come, we must honor such bravery. To Gherifan Arnix!"

"To Gherifan Arnix!" they responded, some reluctant, some delighted, while the object of the toast sat blushing with downcast eyes.

"And a glorious alliance," Ebrin added. He drained his glass, then gave his new protégé a dazzling smile. "Together, we'll set this old town whirling."

The Vinculine's new mistress prowled his house, clad in a guardsman's longcoat rosy as her lips, rope-thick plait swinging with each step. Passing through rooms of well-tended treasures, her gaze remained empty and chill. When she came across servants, they melted away before her with all the haste that dignity allowed. Sandhound's sister did not care for their attentions.

Laelis touched objects at random: A plaque of painted ivory. A row of books in gilt wood cases. A porcelain vase tall as her shoulder, oxblood red. A bearded portrait bust carved from dark basalt. But she never paused for long until she came to a small table covered with a rumpled piece of velvet. Beneath the cloth lay an array of miniature figures, exquisitely wrought in glass. An awkwardness in placement suggested that one had been removed.

For the first time, Laelis smiled. She bent for a closer look. The colors were gem-bright: emerald lizard spotted with scattered gold, kneeling bowman in glowing amber, goddess stepping naked from a swirling, nacreous cloud. . . . Laelis scooped the figures up and in one swift movement hurled them against the far wall.

A laugh sounded from the doorway.

She glanced over her shoulder. It was the Vinculine, with a taller man behind him.

"Come here, Laelis. There's someone you should meet. You have something in common." Ebrin grinned. "A destructive interest in glass."

Without haste, she made her way to them.

"My esteemed companion, Laelis." The Vinculine bowed to her. "My honorable colleague in the pursuit of justice, Ser Gherifan Arnix." Another bow.

Gherifan stood beside him, swaying slightly. He was solemnly drunk after a long night spent with Ebrin, lingering over wine after the other guests had gone from Arnix House and Berec retired to his bed.

"Sera. Enchanted." In lieu of a gesture that might topple him, he placed hand upon heart.

Laelis observed the stained bandage. "You were injured?"

"Was I? Ah, that." A sheepish look. "It's nothing."

"A noble act of defiance," Ebrin corrected. "Admirable, for all it was mis-aimed." The hours of drinking had brightened his eyes and brought a slow luxuriance to his speech.

Gherifan was on his way across the room, stepping like a rope dancer suspended high above safe ground, his goal the heap of glass fragments. They caught the light in points and stars, a confusion of colors. Some figures could still be distinguished amid the ruin.

"Now Laelis assaults my possessions for quite another reason," Ebrin observed. "The satisfying crash? Or perhaps the silence, when beauty loses that smug voice which says, 'I am earthly perfection. You can do no better than this.' "

"Like my father, always sure of himself." Gherifan stopped. He was kneeling precariously, one hand hovering over the broken glass. He gazed up at the Vinculine. "Do you think I killed him?"

"I think some villain beat you to it."

A quaking spasm of laughter overtook Gherifan then.

Soft rustle of cloth, and the pad of bare feet. Splendid in her eccentric garb, Laelis stood at his shoulder. She examined him as she'd look at some rare bird trapped in a net, with casual curiosity. "I've forgotten your name. What is it?"

It bubbled up out of the helpless laughter. "Arnix."

"Well, Arnix," the Vinculine declared, "we must find an intact bottle of wine and share one last toast. To the dead!"

"The dead," Laelis echoed, smiling at the drunken boy. Lightly her lips brushed his cheek.

One of Xalycis's greatest actors had once declared: "I am a mirror—fashioned by the gods." The arrogant humility of that statement had always fascinated Gherifan. Now it took on another meaning, as a faith he could hold on to. The man might be weak, but the actor could call upon a hidden strength, greater than himself. Only that thought kept him from running, in fear of what this Gherifan had become. The Vinculine's Gherifan—or Arnix, as Ebrin liked to call him, seeing the whole family's downfall in the son's disgrace.

There was no more pretense of a quest for Aubric's killer.

Gherifan's few tentative suggestions had been brushed aside, in favor of immediate pleasures. The Vinculine was in high spirits these days.

It would not serve Gherifan's purpose to portray the complete victim, ready to crumble at a touch after a few nights' debauchery. What the Vinculine had damaged, he discarded. *I am a mirror.* The answer was there, and the challenge: to become a perfect reflection, never a rival, safe—until the figure in the mirror stepped out, to assume a life of its own. Not now. Not yet. . . .

Tonight's performance would be played to the faint echo of the day's applause, for the Vinculine had given a rousing speech before the Council, warning against foreign interventionists and the outflow of relicts. By now, bazaar scribes would be hawking copies, the ink barely dry.

Ebrin and Arnix lounged in loose robes, watching the smoke coil lazily up from a brazier of snakeweed. The only other light in the room came from the hearth, where cedar wood crackled with blue flame. They were waiting for Sandhound—and the night's other players.

At last there came the clicking of boot heels, like the patter of dew claws (snakeweed made it easy to envision Hound in canine form), and the muted shuffle of bare feet, the clink of an anklet. The door swung open to reveal Sandhound, pale and grinning, one gloved hand on the shoulder of a tall, heavily built woman, the other cradling the head of a half-grown boy. Street whores, the both of them, both naked.

"They know their parts?" Ebrin asked. He was the author of this entertainment.

"Aye." Hound propelled the boy forward. "Go on, say your piece."

With an illiterate's flawless memory, the boy parroted the opening remarks of the Vinculine's Council speech.

Ebrin smiled. "Excellent. Now you, madam."

Massive breasts and belly wobbling, she advanced to the center of the room. In a low, sweet voice, she pronounced a series of raw obscenities.

"That will do." The Vinculine rose, stood for a moment with arms raised, then let them drop. "Together!"

Forceful political rhetoric and gutter filth entwined in an interplay of voices. In the sensory distortions of snakeweed, this duet became at once music and violent sexual act, though boy and woman never touched.

Signaling to Gherifan to remain as he was, Ebrin threw off his robe and strode to the hearth. The firelight flickered across his wiry body, scant as the boy's but triumphantly aroused. His laughter added a third voice to the manic weave of sound. He glanced at Gherifan, whose role was to stand mute, detached, unimpressed, until the performers fell silent—and then to deliver an eloquent, extemporaneous rebuttal. Arnix had not been allowed to see or hear the original speech.

So Ebrin thought, underestimating the resources of a wealthy young man on good terms with most of the household staff despite his obvious dissipation. Gherifan's response had been ready before the cheers had died in Council Hall. Now he could devote his attention to nuances. For all the revel's gross absurdity, Gherifan knew it could end badly for him should he fail to strike the right note. He could give his own speech in two voices, mimicking boy and woman, suggesting the obscene while remaining clothed (like Sandhound, who slouched in the shadows, watching), in a performance whose skill would pass unnoticed, overlooked.

The power rose in him: he became his words.

And the Vinculine was well pleased. "I'll get you a seat in the Council!" he cried. "Between us, we'll fuck this whore of a city till she bleeds."

"Or begs for more." Gherifan grinned. He glanced behind

him. Sandhound had gone, taking his hirelings with him. It was Laelis who stood in the doorway, gazing in with that dead stare he found so unnerving, as though a painted image moved and spoke.

"Ah, my dear." Ebrin beckoned. "Come, choose the winner in our little debating contest."

"Is there a prize . . . and a forfeit?"

Her voice sent a shiver through Gherifan; still touched by snakeweed, he heard it as a rattling of stripped bones. Death stood in the room with them.

The Vinculine's response came after a calculating pause. "The loser's beloved goes to the winner—for one night. Prize and forfeit in one."

Laelis immediately gave her judgment. "Arnix has nothing to forfeit, so he must win."

Ebrin laughed. "Why, of course. And so, my dearest—"

She forestalled him. "Your best beloved lies in a prison house with three companions."

For an instant, his features twisted with raw fury. Had there been a hint of triumph in Laelis's manner, he would have struck her down. Instead he turned his back and squatted before the hearth, hands extended toward the meager flames.

"Perhaps this is an honor I should decline," Gherifan said, hoping the unsteadiness in his voice would be mistaken for intoxication.

The firelight striped Ebrin's bare flesh with shifting light and shadow. When he swung round, his face remained in darkness. "You have earned your prize, Arnix, and you'll get it."

"At the master's discretion." Laelis smiled ironically. "Someday."

Unexpectedly, Ebrin laughed. "Malicious creature. You'd like nothing better than to see us at each other's throats, wouldn't you? Well, you've won nothing tonight. This is

Arnix's grand moment, and he'll have his due. When would you like to meet my best beloved, Arnix? Tonight?''

Gherifan's fear returned in full measure. It was too soon, he wasn't ready! But he would never be ready if he gave in to cowardice. So, affecting a tone of amused nonchalance, he replied: ''This paragon of yours should be prepared for me. Perfection made more perfect, seasoned by a little waiting. Shall we say . . . tomorrow?''

''Splendid idea. And I have another.'' The Vinculine rose smoothly to his feet. ''You can get in training yourself. Spend tonight with my *second* best beloved.''

If the joke was on Laelis, she joined in it agreeably enough. She stood before Gherifan, loosed the sash of his robe, and eased the garment from his shoulders. Her cool hand touched his collarbone, then his chest. ''Sweet boy.''

The Vinculine stood watching. There would be no privacy for Arnix tonight, nor any sleep.

XI

The Mirror

Railu had wheedled and threatened, to no avail. Lodvin wanted Stilpin with him on his return to Cloud House.

"Don't sit at her feet," Lodvin advised. "Walk around the room, keep her off-balance. This time we can't just charm our way around her like Railu did. I need to use the work-rooms."

Stilpin had dealt with grandees as self-absorbed as Margola. He expected Loddy to crumple under the force of her will—but this was a new man.

"Impossible," Margola declared. "I don't want you fumbling through Chityr's things." (She was unaware that he had already taken the notebooks, small and easily smuggled.)

"Isn't it true, sera, that when a man dies intestate, his eldest son inherits? This house may be in your name, but not its entire contents." Stilpin addressed her with cold formality.

Margola was working up to a fine rage when Lodvin cut her off. "Let me show you something, Mother." From his pocket he removed a small wooden box. Opened, it disclosed a complex array of metal gears under glass. A delicate music came from it, along with a modulating sequence of scents— Vuorn's portrait of Margola in miniature, performed to a tune the composer had dedicated to her many years past. The original of the music box, which sat on a table in one of the upper rooms, lacked the perfume portrait. Gravely, Lodvin presented the new box to his mother.

While Margola still marveled, Lodvin said, "Ghosts don't have hands to create or brains to invent, and what's Father without that? Locked in a shrine, he's as dead as if you killed him twice. Let him go, Mother. I have hands, and believe it or not there's a brain to guide them. And I have a name: Lodvin Chityr." He had drawn himself up to his full height and stood gazing down at her with a stern look she had never seen before. Or had—but on a different face, beloved and lost.

She darted an appealing glance at Stilpin, who remained unmoved.

Lodvin held out one large hand. "Give me the keys." A quiet demand with no threat behind it, but grounded in an inexhaustible stubbornness.

Margola's eyes narrowed. "On one condition." She let the silence lengthen, then went on, casually cruel, "You've changed, Loddy, I grant you that, but you'll never take a polish. You have little conversation and less charm—"

"The condition, Mother?" The hand remained out-stretched.

"This gentleman"—a nod toward Stilpin—"shall dine with me each day you use the workrooms. If for any reason he cannot appear, your dancer friend takes his place. So long as you invade my privacy, your friends forfeit their freedom."

An outrageous piece of bravado, of course, when Lodvin held most of the cards, but he did not turn sulky as she had expected. Instead, he broke into an insufferably foolish grin.

"That's a fine plan, isn't it, Stilpin? Bring back some life to this place."

Stilpin's brows rose.

"We can all come," Lodvin went on. "Railu can rehearse here, and 'Bet is sure to feel at home—safe as houses."

Clever, guileless Loddy. While Margola entertained visions of a handsome dancer, Stilpin thought of Moabet hidden in a place where the Helm would not know to look for her and the Vinculine would never think to come.

As Stilpin gave a fractional nod, Margola unhooked the key from its chain and passed it to her son.

"We'll have a fine time," Lodvin assured them. "You'll see!"

Impossibilities multiplied like tadpoles in a pond. A workshop at Cloud House, given over to forbidden exercises of the perfumer's art; a young woman ensconced in a guest room; a Shandar chemic bluntly giving orders to the household staff; Lodvin with his sleeves rolled up, at home with his legacy; and Margola smiling like a schoolgirl, as her world turned upside down.

Among themselves, Margola's guests showed signs of strain. Gherifan Arnix's dangerous game with the Vinculine was never far from their minds—nor was the threat to Moabet. But weariness and worry gave Stilpin an attractively dissolute air. He did not fail to please his hostess. Railu's rarer visits charmed several decades off her age. As for the percept, Margola ignored her, though she took to teasing Stilpin for the pleasure of seeing his cold, efficient shell break open and the young lover emerge, flushed and struggling to control his emotions.

Two days after the guests arrived, Margola found herself the object of universal scrutiny at dinner. They had something to tell her, some demand. She kept the talk deliberately frivolous, dominating the conversation as if their impatient silence were a challenge to her charm. At last, when the table had been cleared, Margola led them to her strongest ground, the heart of Cloud House: her room of masks.

They hung like trophies from every wall, set above shelves of playbooks and other memorabilia. Margola's collection was the work of countless hands. Smooth porcelain glowed beside crudely daubed wood, fragile paper and wire next to gilded brass. The masks were various as their subjects: humans of every degree, maidens, jesters, murderers, kings. Beasts, from a straw-whiskered cat to a lavish hydra. And creatures unidentifiable—a shaman's headpiece of fur, feathers, and bone; a solar disk blank but for its eyeholes. Their empty stares could be conjured into an expectant audience for whatever scene would unfold here. Margola was always at her best playing to a crowd.

Her Thrani boy brought cups of moka and a tray of little cakes, then discreetly departed. Margola left her cup untouched. Its steam rose toward the masks like an offering of incense to an eccentric pantheon. Let the play begin!

The percept fixed that inhuman stare on her and said, ''No doubt you've recognized there's more at stake than an idle mastery of illusion. We have thrown in our lot against a powerful enemy. It's only right that we explain to you.''

Explain she did, lucidly recounting a sequence of horrors and wonders, from the death of the glass collector Murn to the impending fate of Santha Seona, Gherifan's peril, and the urgency of finding a way to prevent the Artifact's use as a weapon. In this dark tale, one figure shone like a beacon fire. He had taken on a role so arrogantly vital, the envy rose in Margola even as she shivered at the prospect of his failure. The masks stared down, not at her but at this bright spirit of a man she had never seen. Gherifan Arnix usurped her imagination.

"Can you see him in your dreams, child?" she asked the percept.

"Spy on his thoughts?" Moabet's expression hardened.

"Such disapproval! The art can hardly be new to you. You've spent all your life looking at naked souls and the world's dirty linen, haven't you? Too late for modesty, my girl."

In charge again, Margola glanced at Stilpin. Stern as the alabaster mask on the wall behind him, he kept his silence. And Moabet Shar seemed deaf to the awkward pause. When she had thought the matter through, the percept spoke. "Yes. I can try to reach him. It will mean using black *khur*."

"Then use it!" Margola rose, secure at the center of the stage. Empty eyes, eyes of glass, living eyes, all were fixed upon her, the unshockable woman, speaker of truth, wise as the windblown hills. "He might need you at this very moment. Get to work—you too, Loddy, and Ser Chemic. Do you want Chityr to look down into this world and see you slacking?"

All jumped to do her bidding, even the distinguished master perfumer who had sat so silent all evening, hurrying to the workrooms as though she stalked behind them with a whip. Their scheme had become hers, and suspense had given way to bustle, just as it ought when the time was ripe. She had learned long ago, there is no greater sin than dullness in a world so gravely in need of passion and adventure. Give the crowd what it wants, then. Stir it up!

With the long tracks of Laelis's nails still fiery on his back, Gherifan was bundled into a closed palanquin, and blindfolded for good measure. Both he and the Vinculine behaved as if this were an absurd game; inwardly, both were nervous as cats. They sat knee to knee, borne in the swaying box by men from Ebrin's private Guard. In the heavy silence of the palanquin, Gherifan's heart beat so wildly he thought Ebrin must hear.

Still blindfolded, he was helped from the box and guided by a strong grip: up some steps, through a door, and down a corridor. (Not a large house, this. Somewhere in the Levels, flat ground out beyond the Low Markets. He had smelled their heady reek along the way: garbage, incense, spice, and blood.)

As they made their way toward Ebrin's "best beloved," there was no sense of a living presence beyond their own passing footsteps. The air was chill, with a faint odor of mildew. A rooftop reservoir? Gherifan stumbled slightly when the grip tightened further and he was pulled to one side. There came the sound of a key in a lock. No guards with them now, just Arnix and Ebrin. It was time for Arnix to turn petulant.

"Is this a hoax? You whip off the blindfold and there's some crone grinning at me with her two remaining teeth? I don't trust your sense of humor, Ebrin."

"You've forgotten, boy, this is Laelis's idea. She likes you."

Blurred recollections of the past night's revels rose in Gherifan's mind. He felt a slight nausea, a lingering shame, at those images of three in a bed by quaking candlelight. He attempted a jaunty smile. "Gods grant me strength."

"Don't worry. There's a creature here, but you needn't fuck it. I have a different manner of surprise for you."

So you believe. Seona and the Artifact—I'm nearly there. Not for the first time, Gherifan wondered if he had gone quietly mad and was rushing toward his doom.

"Chab?" The Vinculine's voice echoed from bare walls. These new surroundings smelled of exotic smoke and stale flesh. The chill of the house deepened here. "Chab! Come out—you have visitors." He murmured an aside: "An incarnation of the Fat God presides over this private shrine. Holy Chab—said to bring luck if you rub the belly, though in this case I wouldn't advise it.''

Without warning, he plucked away the blindfold. Gherifan blinked, dazzled at first by a light that seemed strewn over the room in random splashes of radiance: dozens of simple oil lamps, floating wicks in clay bowls. A shadow moved toward them with a dragging step.

When it entered the light, Gherifan gasped. ''Chab'' wore a fringed loincloth like its namesake, hiding the bonereader's dual sex but leaving bare the great belly, the ambiguous breasts. The skin was sallow—yet it glittered as if dusted with powdered sapphire. Not some whimsical decoration; around the constellations of blue flecks, the flesh was raw. A gleaming wound had spread across the bonereader's brow and cheek. Pain haunted Seona's eyes.

Ebrin too was taken aback. He had neglected his guards' reports while he toyed with young Arnix, and had not known the extent of the bonereader's decline. ''Greetings, Great Chab.''

Seona spat at his feet. Ebrin fastidiously drew back a pace. Then the bonereader giggled. ''It's not catching, more's the pity, Jailor. I did my best to infect your guards.''

''Whatever the Artifact has done to you, it can cure, when you gain its trust.''

''Trust!'' The Santha's voice deepened to a booming baritone. ''Walk into a raging fire, will it listen to your sweet words? It chatters, it roars, it clutches you with its bright fingers until you become one with it!'' A whisper, while the previous words still rang: ''Floating ashes. . . .''

Gherifan choked back pity and horror. Ebrin had given him his cue, and he had a different part to play. ''The Artifact?'' he asked, staring at the Vinculine.

''It's here. The Thrani had it.'' Ebrin sketched a shrug.

"I regret keeping you in the dark, but it's something of a state secret. I couldn't have you rushing off into the Thrani Quarter, howling for vengeance. Imagine the chaos, if all Xalycis knew of their deed—before we are prepared to counter it. And besides"—he indicated the mutilated bone-reader who had remained silent through these calumnies—"you have your vengeance, Arnix."

At the name Arnix, Seona began to shake with a spasm that might have been laughter, or just a random triggering of nerves. The obscene parody of mirth helped to distract Gherifan from the dangerous anger that was rising in him. Not now, not yet. . . .

"Where is the thing?" he managed to ask. "The Artifact?"

"Summon it," the Vinculine directed his prisoner. This party trick was Seona's first achievement.

The Santha's eyes closed. Still moved by faint tremors, Seona spoke one word: "Arkhenazuril."

And through an open door at the far side of the room, a sphere of light came drifting.

"Damn it, he's already there." For a moment, Moabet's voice sharpened, rising out of the slow dream of black *khur*. She took a deep breath of the drifting smoke and sank back into the trance.

"Explain," Dalu demanded. In this state, she would rarely volunteer information.

"Gherifan has let the Vinculine take him to the Artifact . . . to Arkhenazuril. . . ."

In the back of the improvised perfume chamber, Stilpin muttered, "Crazy fool." The words were muffled by his filter mask.

"Yet not Gherifan, not quite," the tranced voice continued slowly. "Holding a mirror."

"What mirror?" Dalu pressed.

"Changing clouds, a passing shadow . . . two become one."

"Pull her out of it, Dalu. She's not making sense anymore."

But the chemic had one last command to give her. "Tell me exactly where in the city they are now."

She had a map of Xalycis in her head. Moabet's reply was admirably precise.

"Then we've got it!" Stilpin cried.

"We've begun," Dalu corrected. "Gherifan will have to make his own luck this time—we can't help him." Briskly he rose and began manipulating the fans, clearing the air of *khur*, while Stilpin went to Moabet. Unwatched, Dalu's lined features crumpled with anxiety. At least Stilpin had the girl to worry about. Dalu could not escape a darker fear: that young Arnix might have vanished forever into the lion's den.

I am a mirror—fashioned by the gods. Gherifan clung to the thought as the Artifact approached. He could see it clearly now. The sphere rested on air, head-high. The seams across its surface stood out like old scars. Beneath the outer shell, there must be unimaginable complexity—layer upon convoluted layer, armed with ferocious wards. But that was for Seona to see; he was blind to such mysteries. As was the Vinculine. Gherifan's stance subtly changed. He took a step forward, with the strutting pride of a small man, the chin-thrust, smiling confidence of one whose power substitutes for beauty. The last of his lingering shame vanished, replaced by luxuriant amusement. There had been fine play last night, after all. Only the Artifact resisted conquest. Stubborn Arkhenazuril.

"Do you know, Ebrin," he said in the Vinculine's own tones, "it might respond to you where Seona failed. Have you tried the *khur* trance? Surely it would recognize its master then.''

The Vinculine gazed intently at the floating sphere.

Gherifan risked a silent prayer: *Let it destroy us both. The clever folk at Vuorn House can deal with it when we're gone.* His features held the same intensity as Ebrin's.

Forgotten, the bonereader sank to the floor, still trembling, hideously smiling. To Seona's vision, Arkhenazuril swarmed with pale fires, tongues and arcs in constant motion as the wards assumed new configurations. So they had always been, but Seona's first confidence had not recognized them as the instruments of death. In the *khur*-darkness, they would expand, become enfolding wings of light. Though they had brought only destruction, still Seona found them glorious.

Ebrin was speaking. ''Shall we share, then, Arnix? Brothers in magic as we have been brothers in love? We hold much in common.''

'' 'Common'?'' the mirror-image mocked. ''*Extraordinary*, I should say. Gentle Laelis and elusive Arkhenazuril.''

The Vinculine laughed. He beckoned to the Artifact. ''Come, my sweet. Can you take on two at a time?''

Unseen, except by the bonereader, the balefires flared and changed color. But Arkhenazuril remained fixed in place as though the air held it in a firm grip. It listened to its own voices.

Brothers in magic, Ebrin and Arnix were now so closely attuned, Gherifan was not sure which had said, ''Seona, light the *khur*.''

But the rapport shattered when the Santha tried to rise and collapsed, howling. The multiplying crystals had finally reached Seona's eyes.

Horrible that howling, now a man's anguish, now a woman's scream, now wholly animal, brute pain loud enough to bring the guards at a run. The Vinculine flung back the doors to admit them and snapped, "Subdue that creature. It can't harm you, but I fear it's lost its mind."

Warily the two armed men closed in on the Santha, casting nervous glances at the Artifact. Then, perforce, they forgot it in the struggle to overwhelm Seona, who struck out in the rage of blindness, madness. Finally one man swung a truncheon with all his strength, and the bonereader collapsed.

"Take it to one of the back rooms. Set some chains on it—and a gag," Ebrin directed. When they had done his bidding, dragging their prisoner gingerly as though it were a week-old corpse, he turned to Gherifan. "What a disappointing ending to our visit." For once the urbanity seemed forced. Much of the Vinculine's hope had rested on Santha Seona.

Gherifan was suffering an equal disappointment, awkwardly mingled with relief. Death had brushed them with its shadow, then retreated like a coward. He could muster no more than a shrug and an unconvincing grin. "Another time."

The relief swelled in him when Ebrin picked up the blindfold and tied it in place again. Wordlessly they left the chamber, then the house. Thank the gods, he was alive! But Gherifan sobered at another thought. He did not know if he could summon the courage to face it all again: mirror, Artifact, the final intimacy of black *khur*. Was Ebrin equally afraid? He could no longer tell. The spirit that had possessed him had vanished and the moment of unity seemed impossible now, repugnant. He wanted only to crawl away to some quiet place and sleep.

A midnight search of Vuorn House found the percept gone. Ebrin's guardsmen had no brief to question Etroren i-Vuorn with any show of violence—the Vinculine had dispatched them hastily in the first flush of inspiration, not anticipating that his new quarry might have fled.

They brought him the news with the stoic faces of underlings expecting their master's fury, hoping only to outlast the storm.

Which duly broke. They shuffled like old men as they left the room where Ebrin sat, scowling horribly. No sign of her! Vuorn had suggested she might have left on an outbound caravan "some weeks ago." Weeks. . . .

The Vinculine stared before him, unseeing. This wasn't the day's first bad news. Word had come this morning that the Santha had managed to commit suicide, strangling in its chains. He had to find another intermediary to work with Arkhenazuril. In a city swarming with oracles and priests, forbidden essences and creatures ripe for any game, there must be someone who could take Seona's place. The image of the percept entered his mind again. What a strangely delicious shock it had been when she predicted old Arnix's fate! If she hadn't seemed so frail, overwhelmed by her powers, he would have chosen her before Seona. Had he been wrong? He didn't like the thought of the percept running loose. It niggled, an itch he could not scratch.

As though a hint of snakeweed drifted through the room, Ebrin had a sudden vision of people vanishing like burst bubbles, one by one, seers and illicit chemics touched by some impossible magic. Could the Artifact reach out so far? He shivered, but dismissed the thought. They had run away like Jesimis, cowards all. Forget them! He'd go to the Blue Lion tonight (Innmaster Rodion, another disappearance . . .), to the Lion and its bounty of whores. There were some of them clever enough to ease even the Vinculine of his burdens for a time.

* * *

"They've placed a watch on me," Vuorn said. "Not hard to elude, however. If Ebrin wants to set up a proper tyranny, he'll need better trained men. What an anarchy this city is —and has been since the mages fell, I suppose." His thoughts were darting wildly; the excitement of his escape still animated him.

"The Helm gets new recruits every day," Stilpin put in. "They're flocking to the Vinculine's call. How long before they learn the drill and march off to sack Thranis or Shand, for the greater glory of Xalycis?"

"He won't make a move without the Artifact." Margola spoke authoritatively, as if it were she, not Moabet Shar, who had a bond with Arkhenazuril, a key to Ebrin's most closely guarded secret. "His hands are tied."

"And ours are free?" Stilpin's expression was so morose, Margola could not resist tousling his hair like the loving mother she had never been. That roused a sheepish grin.

"We have Loddy and Moabet, while all Ebrin has is a dead bonereader," Vuorn pointed out.

"He has Sandhound. Hell, he has Gherifan Arnix, if he only knew what that meant." Stilpin was frowning again. The strain of watching Moabet go where he could not follow, into the visions of black *khur*, was beginning to tell on him. "The people love Ebrin. Even Wallwalk dotes on him now."

"Nonetheless, he is a vulgar little man," Margola declared grandly, and changed the subject. "Just what is Loddy up to, camped out in Chityr's workrooms? It's been three days since I last saw the boy. He looked quite *wild* with inspiration."

"Well, he's mapping the Artifact's patterns of energies with 'Bet—looking for a clue to what's wrong with it, or some weak point, I suppose," Stilpin answered. "Then he kept Dalu up half of last night putting together what Loddy calls 'cloaks of invisibility.' Between times, he rummages through the notebooks and the materials.'' A headshake. ''The gods know there's enough of them.''

''Chityr spent orrins like water.'' Margola had a reminiscent smile. ''He called me his Phoenix Stone, since I—not some magecraft—kept him supplied with gold.'' Her expression lost its softness as she returned to the inquisition. ''Have you formed any plans for dealing with the Council?''

''What?'' Stilpin stopped with a glass halfway to his lips, and gave her a baffled look.

''The Council. Plans,'' she enunciated, sweetly precise. ''When you've won.''

''That's a rather premature consideration, isn't it?'' Vuorn suggested.

'' 'The exercise of power is a lifetime's art, an unending dance, to be pursued though your soles rub raw on the bare stones of the city.' '' Margola hissed the lines with half-closed eyes, as she had done every night in the memorable run of *Queen Halakit's Choice*. Once again, they produced a rapt silence better than applause.

But Stilpin was no player general harangued by his monarch. ''If we're not all dead by next month, or next week, ask me again.'' He finished the wine at a long swallow. ''Maybe we'll be left together in a cozy dungeon where we can debate the matter at our leisure.'' He rose with a nod to his hostess. ''Sera, by your leave.''

She waved him away with a gesture of weary disgust. Margola did not believe in failure, doubts, or qualms, once a goal was known. Despite all that a long experience might teach, she believed least of all in death. It had no power to command her, this thing that happened to bonereaders and grandees, perhaps, but never to oneself. Where Stilpin faced a future of shadowy uncertainties, Margola saw only glory ahead. Lifelong, she had bathed in its golden aura, worn it and wielded it. Let the young men fret! She turned her attention to Etroren i-Vuorn. Gazing at him, she could see herself reflected in his eyes.

XII

Powers of Darkness

At first, Gherifan thought he was going mad. Had his encounter with the Artifact knocked his mind off its precarious balance, or insinuated some alien presence into his brain? He lay in bed, drenched in a cold sweat, listening to a bodiless voice that spoke his name.

Then, as though a door had opened into a nearby room, he heard: "He's awake, but he's not responding. Loddy, are we doing this right?"

The percept! Gherifan rose, self-consciously pulling on a robe. He was unshaven and his breath smelled of sour wine. Hardly fit company. . . . Then he called himself by one of Dancer's choice epithets and lay down again. Whatever she was doing, this was no social call. He closed his eyes, tried to relax. *Can you hear me, Sera Shar?* And felt faintly absurd in the ensuing silence.

But the voice returned, close as though she knelt beside him. "Gherifan. Yes, I hear you."

From that moment, it seemed they were simply speaking together in a dark room, like children sharing secrets in the night.

"Gods be thanked, we can talk then," she said.

"How are you doing this?"

"A light *khur*-trance, and . . . it's like recognizing a beacon fire. I saw you with Arkhenazuril, and that taught me something of your mind's configurations. You handled it well. Dangerous, though."

"Don't I know it!"

"You're still in its field."

"What?" His heart began to pound even before she explained.

"Arkhenazuril has a field of awareness—distorted by its madness, yet no less keen for that. It was designed to interact with humans, almost certainly to influence their behavior. Lodvin and I are still arguing about the uses of its energies."

"You're saying that thing followed me back?" He was trembling now. All too easy to imagine the floating sphere extending tendrils of mist and reaching out to find him here in Ebrin's house, the lying player, the intruder. After all, the percept had tracked him down easily enough.

"Yes."

Gherifan sat up, angry and afraid, not really caring if the contact broke. Was that all she could offer him, a blunt *yes*?

"I believe it began to work on Ebrin when first he saw it at Council Hall. A better prospect than your father, from Arkhenazuril's point of view."

When he had worked out what she meant, the force of it struck him. He had never thought to analyze the Vinculine's actions in this way. "So the Artifact corrupted him."

"It roused what was already there."

The experience of mirroring Ebrin was still vivid in Gherifan's mind. He could easily imagine the mage-thing working in him, seeking out the darkness in his own soul. "I'm helpless against it."

"Nonsense. Your tactics were exactly right. You used Ebrin like a shield, and came close to passing through the wards."

"I wanted it to destroy us—and itself. Oh, I was full of the holy fire! But that's gone, percept. I couldn't do it again if you tied me up and dragged me there." A worse thought came to him. "Can it hear what we're saying?"

"Not to understand. Arkhenazuril's own voices are too loud within. It senses your value, that's all. Just be glad there's no mage to guide it. You'd be swallowed up."

Value. Swallowed. "Perhaps you might explain that," Gherifan suggested with a brittle calm—which promptly broke. "Or are you all tease, no delivery?" he added, with a Tumbleside gesture that fortunately went unseen.

After a slight pause, Moabet replied levelly, "I called Arkhenazuril's energies a field. It's two fields, to be more exact. Two souls, flexible, mutable, a double mirror. I don't know how the mages went about making their tools. How scarce were the right kinds of mind? Scarce enough now they'd find few volunteers. Lodvin's father was speculating along those lines, with Margola as his example. If he'd come across you before he died, he might have been tempted to try it. Or maybe they were mages, made nearly immortal as some kind of reward." Frustration in her tone now. "Whatever they were, you share part of it. I think Arkhenazuril senses that."

"Immortality. Ser Arkhen, Ser Azuril." He could imagine how a mage would deal with the Artifact: flattering, adoring with a cynical worship, coaxing out greatness. Poor Arkhenazuril, left to its own devices for so long, starved of prayer and praise. "What do you want from me?" he asked suddenly. "What help can I possibly be?"

Her answer was a long time coming. "You'll act as your fate guides you. As you wish, as you must. Before much longer, the crisis will be here. You're part of the pattern. A key."

If she had been within reach, he would have shaken her, hard. "A key for *whose hand*, damn it? Maybe Ebrin will feed me to the beast and head off for Thranis, banners flying. Why don't you just lock me in a cellar and have done?"

"Gherifan. Your instincts are right, always have been. And you haven't fled the city or done murder, or refused to face danger. Like it or not, you're in the thick of this. However we can be of use, we're with you. Understand, you're not alone."

Yet, when she had taken her oddly formal leave of him, Gherifan had never felt more alone in his life. He stood at his window, silent, until the dawn came.

After enough snakeweed, Sandhound saw the shape of the universe clear in his mind. Sky above sky, the thin blue realms of the honorable dead, and hell below hell, the kingdoms of the wicked. No doubt of his own destiny—he embraced it.

Between the blue and the dark fires, Xalycis was his. It spoke to him now, whispering of percept and maker until he knew without a doubt they were together, and that Vuorn could lead him there. Let the Helm bumble, the perfumer escape them: Hound would follow the track to its end.

And within three days, the perfumer brought him to Cloud House like a burr clinging unseen to the hem of a cloak.

The place looked poorly guarded, for all its eccentric grandeur. He had robbed enough widows in an earlier career to recognize the signs of a woman's house. Masterless—easy pickings.

He returned that night, black clad, blood tingling with the kiss of the Snake, ready to shed his skin and let loose the beast. The house looked like a white bird trapped as it tried to fly away. *Beat your wings, little bird.*

Sandhound slipped around to the back, where he found himself in an unexpected lemon grove, darkness mottled with light from the house's strange windows: crescents, starbursts, crossed blades, all burning blue-white as if the moon lived behind these walls. The place smelled of money.

They kept late hours. He had anticipated that, and it did not bother him. He would be their waking nightmare. Noiselessly, Sandhound glided to the nearest door. Complacent fools! They'd left it unlocked.

Easy as that, he was in. Curving corridor, white as a bone, lit by small, steady lamps. He drew his knife, and the long blade glittered. Though he walked on the edge of ecstasy, Sandhound held on to enough of his wits to be wary. It was strangely quiet for a house where some remained awake. Surely they didn't burn lamp oil for nothing.

When at last he heard voices ahead—a woman and a man—he allowed himself one long, luxuriant stretch to unkink the muscles. Forward then, gliding silent to wrench open the door, knife arm extended, a tight smile on his lips—

As their startled eyes took in that smile, something slammed into Sandhound's shoulders, and he stumbled. Though he recovered quickly, the back of his shirt was drenched, some heavy fluid soaking in, burning cold. His consciousness could not abide it, and fled into darkness. . . .

Lodvin and Moabet donned filter masks and heavy gloves before they touched the unconscious man. Lodvin proved to be a deft hand with a rope (another legacy from Chityr); Sandhound was firmly bound before they began to clean up the residue of the man-trap. Above his mask, Lodvin's eyes were huge, and he kept up a continual chatter, at once nervous and exultant.

"Worked like a charm, didn't it? Maybe it did look a bit

silly, that whacking great bag over the door. I know everyone laughed at the sketch, with that little man drawn in—knocked flat. But it worked. Truly!"

"Yes, Loddy. He jerked the door open just as you said an intruder would. On a night with Stilpin away." Though her features were composed, the percept was very pale. Even with the gloves on, she had been reluctant to touch Sandhound, and she shied away from the knife that had skidded out of his hand.

With the last of the fluid cleaned away, the vapors chased off by the workshop's fan, they removed their protective masks.

"Logic said he would come." Moabet brushed an unruly lock of hair from her face. "I suspect he told no one what he was doing, following Etroren here. For the moment, we're safe. You have my thanks."

Lodvin's expression was uncharacteristically grim. "I have this dreadful urge to kill him."

"You won't," she said.

"I know. Too few vengeful bones in this body of mine." Lodvin looked down at his captive. "But he'll wake up with a powerful headache, Hound will. Serves him right." The thought cheered him, and he made an attempt at a sinister chuckle. "To the dungeons with you, Ser Hound—and no supper!"

For several days, the Vinculine was all public man, engaged in meetings with the Council, galas on Wallwalk, the elaborate congeniality that puts a golden burnish on the dark iron of power. He took Gherifan with him on his rounds, armed with quill and ink for the more delicate negotiations: Ebrin's new private secretary. No matter that young Arnix's hand was as illegible as his father's. He was a tame grandee, and that's what counted.

When Berec i-Arnix crossed paths with his wayward brother at a large evening party, he thought Gherifan had changed much for the better. Well dressed as befitted a man of his station, quiet rather than sullenly withdrawn, stripped of that wearisome sarcasm, this transformed Gherifan was living testimony of the Vinculine's good influence.

Berec said as much to Ebrin, out of Gherifan's hearing, and received a smiling reply: "Good blood *will* out at last, i-Arnix."

So the round went on, a superfluity of talk, drink, and flattery that left Gherifan weary to the depths of his soul. He wondered if the Artifact still retained its link with him. *Rejoice with me, Arkhenazuril. These are the fruits of fame.*

They returned to the Vinculine's house one day just before dawn. The pure, cool air had cleared Gherifan's head, though he felt slightly nauseated with the lingering scents of wine, sweat, and perfume that clung to his clothes. Ebrin was languid, silent, allowing his servants to undress him and put him to bed like a child's waxen doll.

Gherifan did not want to surrender to sleep. He was sitting by the kitchen fire, cradling a cup of moka, when he heard a clatter of boots from the floor above. And something like shrill screaming. He hurried toward the sounds.

There were two guards in Ebrin's room, attempting to restrain a naked, raging Laelis. Her voice had risen from its usual dry whisper to a shriek. "He's lost, he could be hurt! Are you deaf? Don't tell me he wandered off on his own business. Hound has no business that isn't mine!"

The Vinculine was sitting up in bed, too weary to be amused by the spectacle of his mistress in her fury. He seemed relieved to see Gherifan. "Take this creature away, Arnix. Do whatever you like to shut it up. It apparently believes we've mislaid its brother." He gestured to the guards, who pulled Laelis toward the door.

"Where to, ser?" one asked Gherifan.

"Gods. . . ." He scratched at his jaw where the stubble itched. "Take her to the washroom, I suppose, and see if a few buckets of cold water have any effect." He was falling into the Vinculine's manner again. Ebrin's men were used to this by now, and obeyed with the same alacrity they'd give their master.

Gherifan watched, wincing inwardly, as Laelis was reduced to drenched gooseflesh with a sullen glare. Her hair hung lank and dripping.

"All right. That will do. Now, one of those towels—no, two. Oh, hellfire!"

She was whipping her hair back and forth, water spinning out, like a dog shaking itself dry.

One of the guards lost his temper and cuffed her.

"I'll remember that," Laelis said in her ordinary voice. The man shivered, but had courage enough to snap back, "You do that, sister."

A servant was dispatched to bring Laelis clothing. The room remained tense and silent, but for the faint drip of water, until the woman returned. Laelis pulled the gown roughly over her head. Somehow she looked more savage clad than naked.

"All right. Leave us, all of you," Gherifan directed. "Laelis will explain this tumult to me."

There were two stools in a far corner. He set them down where the lamplight was brightest, then gestured to Laelis. Frowning, she sat.

He gazed at her steadily. "I'm at your bidding, sera. Tell me what has happened."

At first she spoke in tight, desperate bursts. Hound had vanished. He was in danger, trapped. She *knew* it, that's all. Then, as Gherifan offered no objections, she lost her defensive air and became merely forlorn, a pitiful figure with straggling hair and pale bare feet on the cold flagstones.

Her account set Gherifan brooding. There must be some link between Laelis and her brother, a more tenuous bond than Moabet had forged when she spoke to him with her mind, but enough to convince Laelis of Hound's plight. While Gherifan could have cheerfully consigned Sandhound to the pits of hell, and Laelis with him, her words gave him an odd sense of kinship. She "just *knew*." Might she know more than she realized?

"Close your eyes and think of your brother," he commanded. "Whatever he feels, you feel. How is it with him?"

Without protest or visible surprise, she obeyed. "Blanket. Warmth. Near asleep." Then her eyes flew open: "His wrists are bound!"

"Does the Helm have him?"

Laelis stood and began to pace the room. "I'll kill them." A whisper like the hissing of a snake. She had not heard his question but was lost in a private fantasy of vengeance.

Gherifan felt a chill in his spine. Sandhound's enemies could be his friends. Might Hound have been caught, somehow, in his hunt for the percept and Lodvin Chityr? *Laelis must not find a way to follow him.*

"Arnix." She was at his side, gripping his arm. "Go with me to the Artifact."

"The Artifact?" he echoed foolishly, taken by surprise. "I don't know the way. I was blindfolded. Ebrin hardly trusts me with that secret."

"Hound told me," she replied dismissively. "You needn't lead—just come along." Her voice softened as she added, "I dream of it sometimes. It speaks to me in words I understand until I wake up. Like knowing what the birds say on the rooftops, or the cats in the back alleys." She gave him a sly, sidelong glance. "Wouldn't you like that, Arnix?"

"It destroyed Seona."

She shrugged. "Seona was old and stupid."

"The Santha was an experienced bonereader. Do you dabble in the dark art, girl?" Fatigue and anxiety had shortened Gherifan's temper. He had no patience left for Laelis's grotesque ambitions.

"Hound and I were raised in the Ashgal Temple, till we ran off. I know the rites of fire and the rites of blood. We spied on everything all the time we were there."

No use arguing with her. Words could not break through that arrogant assurance. Gherifan choked back his anger and forced himself to think. "I can't get you past Ebrin's guards to see the Artifact."

"How many guards?" she asked.

"Two, when I was there."

Laelis laughed. "Two—that puts you in a sweat? If I had an old granny, she could handle a brace of those bastards before the porridge got cold. Leave them to me, Arnix." She rose. "Let's go."

"Must be nearly dawn by now," he put in.

Laelis spat an oath, then muttered, "No daylight down in this hole." Recovering her poise, she swept the damp hair back from her face. In the lamplight, the structure of bones, flesh, shadows, had an unsettling fineness, as though a queen played at poverty.

Her cold fingers closed over his hand, startling him back to full alertness. "Here's the way of it, Arnix. We'll wait for next dark. Or are you too shit-scared to do it?"

"Do what?" he asked warily.

"Ask your Arkhen creature to find Hound. That's what they made it for, isn't it? Spying and prying and murder." She spoke the last words with a childish lilt, like a demonic nursery rhyme.

He did not trouble to correct her. Gherifan was beginning

to see a use for Laelis's obsession. Still, he could not help asking, "Why do you want me along if it's so simple to get in?"

"Magic doesn't go by ones. Its doors have two locks, the blood and the flame, woman and man. Till we get Hound back, I need you, Arnix."

At least she hadn't found her help in the Vinculine. Cheered by this thought, despite the weight of fatigue that was pressing upon him now, Gherifan mustered a brittle wit. "Under your instruction, sera, I daresay I'll soon be quite at home with the powers of darkness."

Laelis gave him a casual glance. "You've met them before, Arnix. I'd say they're already at home with you."

Hound stared at Hound.

"That supposed to be me?" asked the man bound to the comfortable chair.

"No. You're the fool who fell into the trap. *I'm* free," replied the man who stood facing him, with a grin.

To the three observers, they were identical. Vuorn and Dalu, creators of the perfume mask, scrutinized Mask-Hound and found no flaw. Margola, suspicious of any semblance not achieved through a player's skills, tried and failed to pierce the illusion. It disturbed her how completely Stilpin vanished into the mask of the adversary. Among players, none but the mad became lost in their feigning.

Prisoner Hound turned to the chemic. "Who's got a lungful of Ladder Valley dreamstuff, him or me? I don't know what you're pulling, Shandar, but it's shit crazy. You send that poor clown to Ebrin, Ebrin'll eat him for breakfast."

Standing, Hound laughed. "Ebrin'll drink a toast to his pal Sandhound out of your sawn-off skull." He strolled a little closer to his double. "We don't need you. Nobody needs you anymore."

The yellow eyes narrowed. Prisoner Hound shook his head. "They're looking for me now. When they find me, you're dead."

Despite the tough talk, they were fascinated with each other, these Hounds. Free the bound man and give them both knives, they would fight to the death with a fierce joy.

"Have you seen enough?" Margola inquired of her fellow observers.

Vuorn murmured his assent, while Dalu gave a curt nod. They signaled to Mask-Hound, who strutted from the room with one last contemptuous glance over his shoulder.

The moment they were through the door into the adjoining workroom, Dalu caught Mask-Hound full in the face with a fine spray of neutralizing essences. It was Stilpin who emerged, wiping his face on one dark sleeve. Or nearly Stilpin—for some traces of Sandhound lingered about him.

"Sweet gods." He was wide-eyed, breathing like a runner after a long race. He pulled off the black shirt and flung it from him. Dalu trained the spray on his chest.

For once, Margola did not seize the opportunity to flirt with the percept's handsome lover. She was too unsettled by what she had seen. "Vuorn, that wasn't an illusion," she declared. "It was a case of possession. If you'd waited a bit longer, your creature would have picked our pockets and slit our throats. Wouldn't you have?" She rounded on Stilpin.

"I don't know." He slumped on a stool, wanting only to scrub himself till his skin was raw and his soul clean again. Still staring at his black-clad knees, he asked, "Did you guess how it would affect me, Etroren?"

"Moabet did," Vuorn admitted. "Thus her absence today. She did not want to witness what we had done."

"But she did nothing to stop it," Margola said.

"We need whatever weapons we can make or find," Dalu put in. "How will it go with Xalycis if the Vinculine gets hold of Moabet? If he finds a way to rule through the Artifact as the mages did, for centuries?"

"He'd welcome you with open arms. Just bring him a pack of Hounds," Margola replied with exquisite contempt. "Gods, how a tyrant would love a clever man like you!" Then, the picture of righteous indignation, "If Moabet and Loddy have turned their backs on you, I salute them."

"Damn it, Margola, we're running out of time." Stilpin spread his arms in supplication. "This project of theirs, figuring out what's wrong with Arkhenazuril, it could take years. And we have what? Weeks? Days? Until Ebrin finds us and crushes us under his heel."

"As he 'found' his runaway mistress, one Jesimis-nenna?" the actress asked wickedly. "I fear you overestimate the man."

Vuorn winced. Stilpin was drawing breath for a fiery rebuke when the far door swung open and Moabet ran into the room.

"He's made a break."

"Hound?" Stilpin jumped up, alarmed.

She shook her head. "Gherifan. I was fool enough to tell him . . . well, it's too late now." With an impatient grimace, she dismissed regret. "He's found his own kind of invisibility, and he's somewhere out there now."

"Then farewell Hendor Ebrin," Stilpin said with a mock salute.

"I can *see* Ebrin. Gherifan's nowhere near him."

"Sounds like you'd better settle down to think it out," Dalu suggested. "How many places could the boy be?"

"What would draw him out?" Margola asked.

Moabet paled. "Arkhenazuril." Guess became percept's certainty. "He's gone for the Artifact."

They all began to talk at once, a babble of horror, anger, disbelief. At last Vuorn made a brusque gesture. "Enough!

I gather that the matter's urgent. Moabet, what would you have us do about it?"

"Go after him," she said simply.

"What about Mask-Hound?" Stilpin forgot his distaste for the disguise, in his eagerness to be of service.

She ran a hand through her hair. "Oh gods—wear the primaries, I suppose, and bring the secondaries along. If the worst comes . . ."

"Where's Loddy?" Margola asked.

Her question was answered when Lodvin himself appeared, edging through the open door with a heap of shifting darkness in his arms. "I brought all of them. Didn't know how many we'd want."

Margola plucked at her son's burden, drawing forth a length of—of what? An uncertainty in the light, a paradox that she handled with some familiarity. "Chityr made two of these, and we had great fun with them. This one seems different, though." She flung it around her, gestured as though she drew up a hood—and Margola was gone. Disembodied, her voice declared, "What are you playing at, Loddy? I'm *dissolving* in this damnable thing."

"It's perfectly safe, Mother." Lodvin's gaze slid past the vague flaw in the air where she had been, then came to rest apologetically on Vuorn. "I used some essences in the material. Bit of a trespass into your art, I'm afraid."

Bemused, the perfumer took another of the cloaks. "Denial of the senses. Sight, smell. Almost it fools the touch. More than a mask. Ah, clever!"

Dalu was busy reapplying the primary essences of Stilpin's Sandhound disguise with flicks of a perfume wand. Unlike Margola, Stilpin remained perfectly visible—but a friend walking in just then would not have recognized him, while some crony of Hound's would have given him a second glance before shaking his head and dismissing the half resemblance as a trick of the light.

"What'll we do with *him*?" Not-quite-Hound gestured toward the closed door to the room where they had left their prisoner.

Dalu's hands stilled for a moment, then continued in their task of packing the secondaries into a leather pouch. "Leave him. If we don't come back, the servants can let him loose tomorrow."

"Free him?" Margola began to protest.

"Why not?" Dalu asked. "If it's already too late for us."

"Take heart, friend," Vuorn said quietly. "May your gods preserve us."

The Shandar bowed his head, then looked up with a kind of calm ferocity. "And bring our enemies to dust and ashes. Be it so!"

XIII

Arkhenazuril

Laelis did not trouble herself with disguises. "Why should we skulk? It's dark enough, Arnix."

Blue twilight enveloped the city. It was a chill night. The stars seemed to cluster more thickly, shine brighter, above these ill-lit streets where tradesmen were heading homeward. Gherifan and Laelis moved with them, equally anonymous wayfarers.

As he neared the Artifact's hiding place, Gherifan felt his soul hollow out. He could have tasted Laelis's mind with ease, wine from a skull, but he sensed its bitter strangeness and held resolutely aloof until they stood before the doorway facing the Vinculine's guards. Then he slipped an arm around her waist. No need to prompt her. Laelis nestled against him as she greeted the guards with a smile of unfathomable promise.

"Are we late?" she asked. "Is he here yet?"

"We've had no orders—" one man began.

"No orders?" Gherifan raised a brow. "How very . . .

unfortunate.'' Soft, almost lazy, the voice of Hendor Ebrin's shadow. "Then we shall have to loiter on the doorstep.''

Such a mixture of overbred languor and inner toughness, the echo of authority, the delicate display of lust. They could no more deny him than they could bar the Vinculine from his own door. And Laelis's sidelong look roused them to break free of routine—to dare what they might not have dreamed of, moments before.

"Must be all right,'' the second guard suggested. "Wouldn't be here except on his say-so. Wouldn't even know the place.''

"Another fuckin' screwup,'' the first guard muttered. "Pardon my language, sera.'' He waved them in. "We're always the last to know.''

The door shut behind them. Laelis gave a sympathetic nod. With no change of expression, she drew a knife—half-size version of Sandhound's blade, a pretty toy—and the nearest guard collapsed, choking on his blood, before either man knew they were under attack.

Gherifan, weaponless, simply launched himself at the other, who fell with a hard crack of skull against stone. As Gherifan rolled to one side, shaking off an instant's vertigo, the guard made a strange barking sound and his throat bloomed red. Laelis had leaned over and slashed his windpipe.

If the Artifact's closeness had not carried his sense of self away into a cold dream, Gherifan would have crawled to a corner and vomited. Safe in the dream, he rose gracefully to his feet, indicated the open hallway. "Shall we . . . ?'' He could ignore both the blood spattering Laelis's pale hair and the half-satisfied hunger in her heart. Arkhenazuril was waiting.

She stopped to pluck a bundle of keys from one dead man's belt, then went with Gherifan into the expectant silence.

The last time Gherifan had come this way, he had been blindfolded, gleaning what he might from sight and smell. Laelis had only heard of the place at secondhand. Yet they walked unhesitatingly, directly to the one door, and she did not have to fumble to find the right key.

Only a few lamps flickered in the Artifact's chamber. The back of the room was lost in shadow.

"Where is it?" Laelis asked. "Hiding?" She gave a sharp whistle that rang from the bare walls.

Thus summoned, Arkhenazuril came. In the reduced light, its seams resembled old scars crawling across dry flesh. Gherifan felt the weight of its age. His memory resounded with the bonereader's screams. Madness to come here—had it planted the notion in Laelis's mind and lured them like two foolish fish?

The momentary panic ebbed. He had come with a purpose. Cling to that.

Laelis had her own plan. From the pocket of her jacket she drew a small pouch. Kneeling by one of the lamps, she dropped in a lump of coal-black *khur*. Presently it began to smolder. Tendrils of smoke rose, clouding the air like the first manifestation of a ghost. The Santha's fate did not seem to trouble her at all.

Gherifan had expected the *khur*. Relied on it, indeed, for it would preoccupy Laelis and—with luck—focus the Artifact's mad regard on this new supplicant, open to its strange senses as Gherifan would be closed. Not a mirror this time; scarcely a presence. His thoughts stilled.

"Mage-thing," Laelis said, her voice hoarse with the smoke, "where is my brother?"

There was no human listener to hear and pity her desperation. Gherifan Arnix had become one with the walls, the air, the night.

* * *

Invisibility is not the easiest of arts. Dalu and Vuorn reluctantly put aside their cloaks, defeated by a sense of vertigo and what Dalu bluntly called their "old man's clumsiness." Dalu would keep watch at Cloud House, and Vuorn busied himself writing an account of the Vinculine's deeds, the evidence, and the measures they now took against him. Margola, though, quickly learned how to carry herself and keep silent, an accomplished specter.

So there were four of them, mother and son and a pair of lovers, scarcely able to sense one another's presence, hurrying toward a fate not even the percept could foresee.

At the Vinculine's safe house, they found two corpses, a lingering bitter smoke, and silence.

"Damnation," Stilpin said. "Has he turned killer?"

"He doesn't need *khur*. There's someone with him," Moabet replied.

"Laelis. The sister." Lodvin's voice was grim. Since he had donned cloak and hood, absorbing the essences into his skin, Loddy the gawk was transformed. Unseen, he took on a new authority.

There was a faint rustle as Stilpin knelt beside the bodies in the outer hall. "Dead maybe half an hour. Now what, 'Bet?"

Suddenly she was visible, the cloak pooled at her feet. "Give me a moment alone." She stepped briskly from the room.

They waited in silence for her return, their hoods thrown back so they might feel less alone in this house of the dead.

When she emerged at last, Moabet's face was set in severe lines. "Laelis has the Artifact. She's heading for some bolt hole in the Tumbles. I can't find Gherifan."

"Gods." Stilpin winced as though she'd struck him. "Is

he . . . like them?'' He gestured toward the corpses, unable to say the word that filled his mind.

Margola was tougher. ''Dead,'' she rasped. ''Cold meat. Has that damned boy failed us?''

The Vinculine was lingering over Jabel Fivesides's wine at Masquer's Inn when the anonymous message came. Iron Mog sat at table with them, and Khamon Pars, the Master of the Helm. One look at Ebrin's scowl, and Jabel sent the servants from the room.

''Bad news?'' Khamon asked unnecessarily. ''Someone run off with the Treasury?'' The Master, who had been matching drink for drink with Mog, sprawled boneless in his chair. Across from him, Mog loomed cold sober with his eyes on the Vinculine.

Ebrin stood. It was clear that only a great effort kept his voice level, neutral, when he said, ''Get me some men who know the Tumbles.'' He looked from Jabel to Mog to Khamon: the order was general.

But Jabel would not be outmastered in his own inn. ''Spill it, Hendor. My lads don't go in blind.''

A pause, while the color came and went in Ebrin's face. Then a mask of smooth indifference slid into place, eyes hooded, muscles in the jaw at ease. ''Remember the Arnix Artifact? It's been found, apparently, back in the Tumbles. History repeats itself.'' His tone became intimate, confessional, persuasive. ''Xalycis bests us so easily, with her mysteries. Bests and betrays.'' A flickering glance held Khamon still, questions unasked. ''It seems I have been gulled, sers. Or loved unwisely. Sandhound is missing, and his sister has been seen with the Artifact.''

Now the Master of the Helm was allowed to draw the obvious conclusion. ''They murdered Arnix?''

''It smacks of conspiracy, doesn't it? Gain control of the

mages' handiwork, then win the confidence of a public man, report his every move—to whom? I wonder. We must pray their masters aren't already at hand.''

Jabel Fivesides shook his head. ''Damn it, Hendor, they know your weakness for a skirt. My girls aren't enough for you, those Wallwalk bitches aren't enough—''

''I played with fire.'' The Vinculine uttered the hackneyed words straight-faced, but with an edge of sarcasm.

''All right.'' Jabel acknowledged the hit. ''Time we got the Tumbles covered. Mog?''

''I'm on it.''

''Fancy a wager, Fivesides?'' Khamon offered. ''My men'll take the prize while your bully boys look for their own arses.''

The Helms Master lingered while Mog went on his way. Jabel was quite willing to oblige him. Ebrin watched for a moment, gave his first genuine smile since the note had arrived, then strode from the room, thoughts of Gherifan Arnix fiery in his mind. He had no doubt who was behind this disaster. None at all.

Trails ran through the Tumbles now, where there had been only ancient chaos. The relict hunters had left their marks on shattered walls, set up crude lean-tos, built fires. Few remained to scavenge now in the worked-out pits. Neither greed nor desperation could make this place more than a thing to be endured, exploited, and abandoned with all speed.

Yet just on the edge of Laelis's vision, proud towers rose to the starlight. Soot-streaked rubble drifted like mist and became pale marble. Reality was timeless. No! From the confusion of her thoughts, urgency returned—she must find Hound! The *khur* vision had shown him here, a muffled form whose mind she could no longer touch, but whose presence was familiar as her own skin. She stood with the Artifact in her arms, sensing the world through its field, searching the ruins. Then the towers rose once more and she was lost in the mages' city, in the endless past.

"Laelis." He hung above a shining fountain, suspended.

When she blinked, Sandhound was standing on the remains of a collapsed wall. He smiled at her.

In her relief, she forgot to wonder how the magic had brought him, without help from treacherous Arnix, without the joining that her gods demanded. Enough that Hound was here. Laelis brandished the Artifact like a trophy. "See what I've brought you!"

"Clever girl." He held out his arms. "All ours now. Give it here."

Almost she did as he asked. A tremor in his voice stopped her. Why should he show fear now, in the moment of their triumph? "Arnix has run away," she said, with the briefest of glances toward him.

"Then forget him."

"Nearly did the old rites tonight. Looking for you. Might not have been such a bad thing, with Arnix. Better than Hendor. Better than you, maybe." Laelis manufactured a lascivious smile, held on to it like a lifeline as she waited for his rage to erupt, the killing rage she had turned against so many discarded lovers—waited in increasing anxiety as Hound stood frowning, strangely silent.

"What have they done to you?" she whispered. Her grip on the Artifact tightened. "Where were you, brother?"

He responded with a Tumbleside gesture, bared arm, clenched fist, and a jaunty grin that was all Hound—and none of him, for this was a stranger looking back at her. The air quivered and blurred around him, as though the lantern in his hand had set him alight. His falseness would burn like paper.

Laelis stared at the image of Sandhound with a sudden and

absolute malevolence. Where she touched the Artifact, there was a play of sparks.

"Sister." The voice came from behind her.

Startled, she swung around.

"Sweet sister." Sandhound spoke, yet Sandhound stood speechless.

Laelis took a step toward the tilted rock slabs from which the voice had come. Fire flickered in the Artifact's seamed shell—the faint radiance fell upon shadowed ruins, emptiness. When she turned back to face the lying ghost, all the devastation of the mages' city, the empty aftermath of chaos, lay in her eyes. "No," she whispered.

Stilpin, false Hound, sank to his knees, appalled.

The disembodied voice spoke in his stead: "Arkhenazuril."

As he uttered the word, Gherifan gave himself up for dead. The Artifact would know him now, stripped of his disguise as surely as Stilpin had been revealed by his moment of fear. Arkhenazuril's strength was drawing in upon itself, power distilled and implacable. What would it feel like when it swept down to claim him for its own? The air smelled of lightning.

A bootsole grated against a loose stone, and there came a muttered oath. Mog's men crept toward the uncanny radiance that surrounded Laelis: five Tumbleside toughs with the disciplined brutality melting away from them at the sight of what they'd come for. Near the edge of the light they stopped, staring as Gherifan stared, and Stilpin, in the presence of a miracle. Laelis had become one with the light, translucent, a form breathed into glass. The Artifact's brilliance was clouded with crimson, a swelling stain.

Don't look at it!

Gherifan and Stilpin obeyed the percept's warning instantly, crouching with their hands against their eyes while afterimages flashed pale before them. Nearby, Lodvin crouched with his head down, one arm around his mother's thin shoulders. Confused, Mog's men did not turn away quickly enough. And six guards from the Helm hurried toward the light with no thought but wonder.

Only Moabet knew the full danger and dared it, forcing her mind to stillness while her heart raced. Two men began the fighting, rushing upon each other with drawn swords. Then their comrades joined in—forgetting allegiance. Mog's men wielded cudgels and blades against Tumblesider or Helm guard, whoever was to hand, each man the enemy, all fighting alone. With cries of battle fury, grunts of pain, they fought for their lives. Men fell . . . yet the battle was not diminished. What less than a dozen began, a score continued. Their silhouettes crossed, strained, cast sprays of blood against the light as veins opened, and the light was richly red.

A score of fighters? A hundred, more. They swarmed in open plazas, forced their way down barricaded streets, dodged rains of fire—green, whistling sparks arcing down to explode in thunder. Corpses lay where they had fallen or were shoved aside by circling fighters clearing their own killing ground. Many of the fallen had terrible wounds, flesh open to the raw spill of life. None wore armor. For all their savagery, these were oddly unschooled warriors. The first solitary madness had passed: once more, allies could be seen. Two yelling men in blue robes defended an elaborate fountain against all comers, like a pair of its statues come alive. Another pair stood back to back, struggling to remain in step as they lashed the air around them with steel-tipped rods. Nearby, a wild whitebeard flung off his cloak, a spill of black brocade and gilt, the better to grapple with an enemy who had already stripped naked. Mages. These were mages, at war without benefit of their magics. Driven mad by the madness of their highest achievement, Arkhenazuril. Not ghosts but memories made flesh. Where were their armies? Half a world away, extending an empire that would shake itself apart.

Moabet flinched as a man with a long, curved knife raced past her, but his passage did not even stir her cloak. She was the ghost here. And the others? Invisible still; safe, she prayed. *Stilpin?* There was a stirring to her right. The battle had moved past them, so with infinite caution she went to him. He seemed almost a stranger, half Sandhound still, until he reached out blindly, found her shoulders, and clasped her in a desperate embrace. From the empty air beside him came a murmured question: "Safe to look now?"

Yes, if you must.

Lodvin and Margola were close by. Moabet could hear a hiss of indrawn breath as they saw the carnage. Then Margola asked, "Where's young Arnix?"

Gherifan lay in the grip of nightmare, smelling the stink of blood, hearing the inhuman sounds of the killing field all around him. At any moment, he expected to feel cold steel, then pain, then nothing ever again. Or at the very least the casual kick of a boot as some warrior stumbled over him in the shadows. His continuing survival became a source of wonder, then an itch of curiosity, and at last he raised his head. Two bodies lay nearby. One of Mog's men—he knew him, Eskke was the name, the joker of the company— sprawled grotesque in death, grinning with a final rictus. The second corpse . . . Gherifan stretched a hand to touch the knife still locked in its fingers, and encountered only rough stone. He looked around him wildly, reaching out like a man struck suddenly blind. But for Eskke's corpse, he was alone. Mages, blood, the dying glory of old Xalycis, drifted away in tatters of smoke on the wind. At the center of the ruinous battlefield, the Artifact flickered fitfully, hovering above a soot-streaked bundle from which emerged a woman's hand, palm upward, charred almost to the bone. Laelis too remained where she had fallen.

Gherifan turned sharply at the sound of a laugh from the shadows some distance away. Three dark figures stood in the lee of a shattered wall.

"The creature seems to have defended itself vigorously," Hendor Ebrin observed. "Fortunate that we took our time getting here." He moved another step forward.

One of his companions shifted uneasily. "We don't know it's safe now, Illustrious."

"Are you safe, creature?" Ebrin addressed his wayward possession boldly enough, but not by name. "Or would you prefer to slaughter every living thing in this city?" He added, with a half smile, "I admit, the idea has a certain appeal." Shaking off his worried guards, the Vinculine strolled closer to the dimming sphere and the body over which it hung. His smile died. "You." Giving Laelis's corpse a vicious kick, he cried, "Where is he? Where's Arnix?"

"Here." Gherifan rose from his hiding place. Grime blotched one side of his face and his tunic was a ruin, but his gaze burned steady, fixed on the Vinculine. "Come for your toy?"

"An Arnix toy, perhaps. My weapon."

"Whistle it up, then." Gherifan moved forward, his shadow flowing across the stones. "Give it some commands. Wield it, Ebrin. Or are you afraid?"

"With guards at my back and an unarmed boy posturing before? Pity you aren't a Shandar, Arnix, or I should bid you dance for us. Fit ending for your little comedy."

"Give me a set of blades, I'll put them to good use." Gherifan pulled off his tunic and tossed it away.

"One blade was enough for your father." Ebrin drew his knife. "It will do for the son." He made as if to yield it, then gave a mocking grin. "I'm a slave to habit, you see."

Gherifan responded with a contemptuous Lowtown shrug, half turning his back to the Vinculine and his men. In the silence that now fell between them, he heard a rustling like a passing breeze. The percept and her invisible companions were whispering together. Had he sent them into a panic? Perversely, the thought calmed him. As his heartbeat steadied, an image entered his mind. "Ghosts walk these ruins." He tilted his head. "Can you hear them? They laugh at us —two snarling curs wrangling over a bone." Gherifan's features sharpened; it seemed he attended more closely to the spirits. "They grow sad again, and murmur of the lord who led them to their deaths. His name was Arkhenazuril—a creature with two hearts."

At the sound of the Artifact's name, Ebrin stiffened, but the hovering sphere did not move or change.

"Two hearts," Gherifan continued. "One was a conqueror's, savage and clever. The other craved silence, stillness, peace that charms time to sleep." His voice hardened, with a hint of irony. "A peace worth fighting for. So Arkhenazuril went to war—heart against heart—and his men divided according to their natures, two factions bitterly at odds." A sad headshake. "The ghosts know now that only fools heed the counsels of madness. A lesson Arkhenazuril has failed to learn in all the long years since. Immortal Artifact, perpetual kingdom." Arms extended, he indicated the surrounding devastation. "If only the ghosts were less insolent, the intruding mortals not so damnably predictable."

"Ebrinarnix." It was the Artifact that spoke, in a voice dry and chill and old as the wind.

The Vinculine's face spasmed with some unidentifiable emotion, then grew still. His men were pale with shock.

Gherifan gave a slight nod of acknowledgment, as to a peer. "Lord Arkhenazuril." The role of tale-spinner, prophet, had captured him utterly, and he stood at his ease before the mages' last creation.

"Touch," the Artifact declared—commanded? And again, "Touch . . ." the word fading like a sigh.

"Shall we join hands in amity?" Ebrin inquired, brows raised. "How would you interpret it, Arnix?" Casually sheathing his knife, he examined his spread fingers. "What are the odds? Would we merge like lumps of tallow over a fire, or survive to carry on the struggle? We *have* struggled at close quarters, in the past." Only the barest flicker of his eyes indicated Laelis's corpse.

The ruin that had been a woman lay pitilessly revealed, for the Artifact's radiance had leaped to a new intensity. Around the body, every crack in the stones seemed a black abyss, each grain of dust edged with diamond. The air was brittle with electricity; Gherifan's hair rose in a crackling fan.

Hollow-faced, the Vinculine set aside all mockery to mutter tightly, "The damned thing's out to kill us. Truce?" His guards had backed away so far they could not possibly save him from an attacker. In moments, they would run for their lives. He stood with empty hands, his anxiety evident. As Ebrin reached toward Gherifan—beseeching?—his palms filled with glory-fire. "Listen to me, Arnix."

Gherifan took a half step back as the Vinculine approached him. It was not enough. Ebrin's open hand thrust hard against his chest, over the heart, and a spark snapped like breaking bone. The jolt slammed through Gherifan, sending him flying—to be caught in a firm grip.

Ebrin himself had staggered at the force of the contact. When he retained his balance, he glanced toward what should have been a man struck senseless and saw instead an apparition of weird majesty, gazing back sternly from a gathering of wraiths.

Dust clung to the cloaks of invisibility; in the Artifact's harsh light, they gleamed. Only the faces were dark voids beneath the overhanging hoods. Two of the wraiths flanked Gherifan like wings; two others stood behind him.

The Vinculine drew a long, shuddering breath. "The demons gather to receive you," he managed to say. "Or have your dead, enlightened mages come to welcome you? Have I killed you after all, Arnix?"

One of the specters drifted toward him. Ebrin's bravado gave way to fear. "What do you want?" he cried.

"Vinculine," a remote voice answered. "Master of Xalycis." It grew stronger, harsher. "Spiller of blood." Then sweetened. "Child."

A wary hope dawned in his eyes. "Heir to your powers, Mage?"

"To all that is mine." The wraith turned, beckoned. "Arkhenazuril."

Obediently, the Artifact approached. Ebrin had to slit his eyes against its glare. The night smelled of burning.

"Reach out. . . ."

He could not tell whether Artifact or wraith spoke, but now he understood. He must grasp the cold fire, as his new mentor met him there.

Behind them, Arnix was struggling against the other ghosts, desperation in his face. That was enough to spur Ebrin to a decision. "Yes," he said, and extended his arms to the floating sphere. There was a gentle pressure on the backs of his hands, like a woman's caress, soft gloves. Jesimis. Laelis.

A cry, a woman's name, echoed among the ruins as Hendor Ebrin and the spirit plunged through the surface of the sphere into a howling chaos of light, and were gone.

"Margola!" Lodvin shouted, a moment before the glory engulfed her. "Mother!"

Stilpin stood with Moabet in his arms, his eyes closed, whispering a childhood prayer over and over. "Dear gods, kind gods, merciful gods."

Gherifan remained numb, afterimages smeared across his vision. Gradually, the meaning of that first despairing cry penetrated his consciousness. He felt a belated thrill—had the Red Goddess herself come from the pantheon of players to rescue him? He turned, to hear Lodvin Chityr's raw weeping, and realized the vision had been flesh and blood. Sweet gods, where was she now? Suddenly his legs would not support him; Gherifan fell to his knees.

The brilliance faded like a receding tide, leaving strange, random sparks to float for a moment before they sank to nothing. At last the night returned. Only starlight silvered the Tumbles.

There came a homely clink of metal, a faint popping, and Lodvin held up a small, feebly glowing lamp. He had cast off cloak and hood. Rubbing a hand roughly over his eyes, he came to crouch beside Gherifan. "Do you see it?"

"What? No."

"There." Lodvin's long arm, bony fingers, indicated the place. A fine coating of ashes lay over an object half buried in the rubble. It might have been a stone, or a skull. Its surface absorbed the lamplight, giving back no reflections. "All of them are there. Arkhenazuril, Ebrin . . . Margola."

"Dead?" Gherifan asked, and could have bitten his tongue an instant later for saying it. This was Margola's son!

It was the percept who answered. "Sleeping."

"Who—?" Gherifan began, and could get no further.

"Who won? Who survives?" she completed for him. "Too soon to tell. Even the mad voice is stilled."

Lodvin's hand hovered near the Artifact's dark surface, not quite touching. "A new soul could be forming."

Compounded of Ebrin and Margola, or whichever of the

two proved strongest, and laced with Arkhenazuril's insanity. Gherifan shivered. "Bury it deep, while we still can."

"That would be much the greater danger." Moabet moved into the circle of lamplight, Stilpin close behind. Like Lodvin, they had put aside their cloaks. What was invisibility, beside the need for human comfort?

Gherifan wrapped his arms around his chest, and the fact of his own continuing existence astonished him, driving away some of the fear. Alive. . . .

Stilpin broke into his reverie. "It's yours now, Arnix. Or your family's—stolen and recovered, that simple." Seeing Gherifan's uncomprehending stare, Stilpin added, "The Artifact will be returned to Arnix House."

"Berec's problem," Gherifan muttered. He was shivering again.

Moabet turned her grave gaze upon him. "I think not."

"What do you mean?"

"Some power waits in trust for the true heir. They once called its keeper the Bound King."

Gherifan Arnix shook his head wildly. " 'True heir'? Ridiculous. Not me."

For answer, the percept smiled.

TALES OF THE IMAGINATION
— from —
GREG BEAR

Here are stunning excursions beyond the frontiers of the human mind from the Hugo and Nebula Award-winning writer—and today's hottest young talent in science fiction.

❝ His wonders are state-of-the-art. ❞

—*Newsday*

- ☐ **THE WIND FROM A BURNING WOMAN**
  (E20-846, $4.95, USA) ($5.95, CAN)
- ☐ **ETERNITY**
  (E20-547, $3.95, USA) ($4.95, CAN)
- ☐ **TANGENTS**
  (E21-044, $4.95, USA) ($5.95, CAN)

**Ⓦ Warner Books P.O. Box 690
New York, NY 10019**

461